XY

Shanta Everington's *XY* – joint winner of the Red Telephone Books Young Adult Novel Competition – is her second young adult novel. Her first was *Boy Red*, published by Musa Publishing (Euterpe Imprint) in 2013. Shanta is the author of five published books, and her poems and short stories have been accepted for publication by various small presses, with a story shortlisted for The Bridport Prize. She has had all sorts of jobs in the past, from baking vegan muffins and working as a private tutor to appearing as a guest agony aunt and running a teen sexual health helpline. With an MA in Creative Writing with distinction, Shanta currently teaches Creative Writing with The Open University in London. Shanta lives in London with her young family.

Visit www.shantaeverington.co.uk
or follow @ShantaEverAfter on Twitter.

XY

By Shanta Everington

British Library Cataloguing in Publication Data

A Record of this Publication is available from the British Library

ISBN 978-1-907335-32-7

This edition published 2014 by The Red Telephone Manchester, England

1

Jesse watches through the smeared kitchen window as Randy plays football in the back garden with Zeus. Her brother's face is red and shining with perspiration and concentration as he tackles Zeus, before skidding on a muddy patch and ending up sprawled across the grass.

"Yes! Yes! Come on!!!" shouts Zeus, grinning as he punches the air, shaking droplets of sweat everywhere. He bends over laughing and then he looks up at the window, catching Jesse's eye before she looks away into the washing up bowl full of suds, feeling heat creeping across her chest.

"He's a proper teenage boy your brother, isn't he?" says Jesse's mother, Ana, smiling to herself as she hands Jesse a tea towel. "All rough and tumble. I'm so pleased for him that he has finally become himself."

Jesse feels her shoulders tense up as she fingers the green checked cloth.

"Thanks for dinner, Mum," she says, not meeting her mother's gaze as she starts drying the dishes. "The lasagne was lovely. I should go upstairs and do some revision once I've finished this."

"I can teach you how to make it if you'd like?" says Ana, beaming at her daughter. "Maybe at the weekend, when you've not got so much school work to do?"

Jesse doesn't want to learn how to make lasagne. Or shepherd's pie or pasta bake. She doesn't want to learn to cook or study needlecraft or budgeting skills or any of the Female Life Skills on the syllabus. She doesn't want to play football either. She doesn't know what she wants. It was so much easier before. When she wore white and yellow and green and grey and played with trains and dolls at home, when Randy and Jesse shared everything.

When they were the same. Before Ana took them to see Maya and they moved into their first flat, next door to the old man who smelled of urine. When she didn't have to pretend she'd made a decision. She feels the corners of her mouth quivering as her mother stares into her face.

"Oh Jesse, don't worry," says her mother, rubbing her shoulders. "Your turn will come when you are ready. How are you feeling about things now, darling?"

Jesse shrugs her shoulders and tries hard to smile but somehow she can't quite manage it. Her mother takes the plate Jesse is busy drying out of her hands and places it on the scratched wooden work top.

"Don't worry, darling. I only ever want you to be happy. You've got to be ready, Jesse. Remember what happened to George."

Jesse nods. She has heard the story of Uncle George so many times, it is etched on her brain, like a recurring nightmare.

"I think Zeus might have a crush on you," says Randy over breakfast the next morning.

The family are in the kitchen, sitting around the big, old, oak dining table, a hand-me-down from one of Ana's friends. Most of their belongings are cast-offs. They are used to relying on the charity of others connected to Natural Souls. Ana has set the table with cereal, orange juice, toast and home-made preserves.

"Shut up," says Jesse, spooning muesli into her mouth.

"Seriously. Didn't you notice the way he kept watching you yesterday when you came out into the garden with your tight top on? I don't think it was just your lemon ice lollies he was drooling at!"

Jesse feels her heart beating a little faster. Zeus is nice, she thinks, but nothing can happen. Zeus is one of the Nine Per Cent. He wouldn't want her. At least not until afterwards. If she goes through with it.

"I know you like him!" continues Randy in a sing-song voice. "Don't worry, I won't tell him your secret!"

"Randy," says Ana sharply, pouring milk into her bowl. "Don't wind your sister up before school."

"I'm not!" protests Randy, rocking his chair backwards and stuffing toast into his mouth. "I'm just saying!"

Jesse carries on eating, feeling her cheeks burn.

Randy gets up from the table and whispers to Jesse on his way out of the kitchen, "He likes you, he likes you!"

Once her brother is out of earshot, Jesse turns to her mother.

"Mum, can I ask you a question?" she says, playing with her spoon, turning it over and over and watching her reflection morph into something grotesque.

"Anything," says Ana.

"How old were you when you had your first boyfriend? I know it was different for you. You weren't born like us but…"

"I was fifteen," replies Ana without hesitating. "The same age you are now. His name was Jack. He was a friend of my brother's too. He was born like you but he was a boy by the time I met him. It didn't last, of course."

"What happened?"

"You mean why didn't it last?" asks Ana, absent-mindedly picking crumbs up off the table. "We were just kids. First love. It wasn't even love. When George died, well… Jack's family moved away. It's just as well or I wouldn't have met your father and there would have been no Randy or Jesse."

She looks up at Jesse with a bright smile. Sometimes Jesse wonders what lies beneath her mother's happy face.

"I wish Dad was here," says Jesse. "I wish he hadn't left us."

"I know, darling, but we have to be strong for one another. Think about what I said about seeing Maya again soon. Now, you don't want to be late for school, do you?"

Jesse gets up and takes her plates to the sink before grabbing her school bag and heading over to school. Today she has history, biology, religious education and sex education. It will not be a good day. Her bag weighs heavily on her shoulder. She thinks about the text books it contains and what they are teaching her.

"Ah, Jesse, so glad you could join us," says Mr Hope as she slips into her biology class five minutes late, after a last minute visit to the toilets to make sure she looks right.

"Sorry, sir," comes her feeble reply. She feels her school dress stick to her back as she finally removes the heavy bag and sits down at her desk.

Jesse looks around the classroom at the other girls. Debra Simmonds is painting her fingernails under the desk. But she isn't like Debra, is she? All the boys want Debra because everyone knows that Debra was born pure. She is one of the Nine Per Cent like Zeus. Jesse isn't like Debra. She isn't like the other girls, either. The assigned girls. What if they find out what she is? She wonders how Randy is getting on over at the boys' school. It is all right for him, now he's had the operation. But Jesse is scared. She doesn't know if she can go through with it.

Artemis smiles at her, through her spidery black fringe. They weren't friends before. But since Randy started going out with her it seems that Artemis wants to hang around with Jesse all day.

"Everybody turn to page one hundred, please," instructs Mr Hope.

Jesse knows what is on that page and she doesn't want to look at it. The human reproductive system. But she has to. It is the same in the other classes; lessons all tell her she is wrong. Her mother is wrong. She wishes it had been done to her when she was born, like everyone else. Why did her mother make her have to choose when?

"Hi," says Artemis, as they walk to the lunch hall.

Chairs scrape along the floor and the cutlery clatters. The air thick with the smell of over cooked food and teenage hormones. Jesse isn't hungry, not after looking at those diagrams all morning.

"Randy says Zeus likes you," says Artemis, flicking back her long, black hair as they queue up for their food.

Jesse can see four tiny holes in Artemis's earlobe, where she has taken her studs out for school.

"I dunno about that," mumbles Jesse, wishing she could be on her own again, as usual. She normally avoids conversation whenever she can, sits in the corner gulping down her lunch, pretending to read a magazine, flicking idly over the fashion pages full of celebrities that all look the same and scanning the problem pages to see if there is ever a question from anyone like her. But there never is.

"No, he really does, he told Randy and everything. He wants to go out with you. I know he looks confident and everything but he's really quite shy. So, he's sort of asked Randy to ask me to ask you out for him!"

Jesse freezes as the dinner lady with luminous blue eye shadow spoons vegetable curry onto her plate.

"Don't you like him?" persists Artemis, grabbing an orange juice and passing one to Jesse.

Jesse shrugs and picks up her cutlery.

"He's gorgeous and really clever. What's not to like?"

"Maybe I'm just not ready for a boyfriend," says Jesse, as Artemis follows her to her usual table in the corner and sits down.

"Oh, I get it," says Artemis, waving her hands about.

"You're scared! You're scared about having your first boyfriend. What, have you never kissed a boy before or something?"

Jesse bites her lip and slowly shakes her head.

"What, never?" asks Artemis, holding her spoon mid-air. "Not even with mouths closed? What about at the youth club disco? Come to think of it, I never saw you dance with anyone. Gosh, girl, I've got some work to do with you! Stick with Auntie Artemis and I'll soon have you coming out of your shell. I like a challenge."

Artemis beams at Jesse as she tucks into a piece of naan bread. Jesse smiles and picks at hers. It would be good to have someone to talk to. She can see why Randy likes being around Artemis. She's bubbly and warm and seems to know what to do. Randy was inexperienced like her before Artemis but now look at him.

"You're right," says Jesse. "I am scared."

But not for the reasons Artemis thinks. She must never find out the truth.

2

"Right, I'm off now, kids," Ana calls from the front door. "Are you sure you'll be okay on your own for a couple of hours?"

"Mu-um," groans Randy, appearing in hallway, "We're fifteen and sixteen, not five and six!"

"Well, okay, keep an eye on your sister for me, would you?" she asks, slinging a lilac coloured cardigan over her arm. "She seems a little vulnerable right now."

"Whatever," sighs Randy.

Jesse sits on the edge of the green sofa in front of the television, half watching the news. A class of school children in the north have been struck down with food poisoning. A local MP has resigned after his affair with his secretary came to light. All the usual things. The prime minister's face appears on the screen, his skin pale and clammy, his hair in an exaggerated quiff. Jesse is sure he didn't look like that when he came into power. Every day, his skin seems to get greyer, his quiff bigger, as though he is turning into a caricature of himself.

"We believe that the family unit is the basis of a stable society. Family is at the heart of all our policies, be they health, education, employment or crime prevention. It is vital that this country gets back on track in promoting The Family. This is why we have introduced the new tax breaks for couples with children. With fewer people able to have children in today's society, it is vital that we all work together to support those who can, to raise the next generation of society…"

"Here, here!"

As the sound of his speech drones on, Jesse tries to push her RE homework question to the back of her mind but it keeps flashing before her eyes like subtitles on the screen. The essay doesn't have to be in until Monday but she knows she would have nothing to write even if she had a year to complete it. Nothing that Mrs Pritchard would want to read. She will copy a sermon off the Internet. "God created men and women as different but equal members of society. Discuss."

The prime minister's face has been replaced by a glamorous, young newsreader wearing cerise lipstick and a black and white checked jacket with pearly buttons. She is talking about a new nature reserve that has just opened. Jesse focuses on the image of a bird, its large pale cheeks and tall, flattened, brightly-coloured bill, watching it fly across the screen, its distinctive black head leading the way. She wishes she was a bird.

Cerise lipstick woman is talking again.

"In breaking news, a man and two women, believed to be in their late thirties to early forties, have been arrested on suspicion of facilitating illegal births. They are thought to be members of the controversial group, NBM, Natural Baby Movement, which encourages women to conceal their pregnancies and give birth illegally, avoiding Compulsory Gender Assignment, leaving their babies as intersex people with both sets of sex organs. The identities of those arrested have not been revealed. The police are working closely with all authorities to crack down on this illegal underground ring…"

Jesse sits bolt upright and thinks of her mother, her heart pounding in her chest. What if…? The chime of the doorbell makes her jump. Could it be the police? She darts to the window to peer through the curtains as Randy's feet pad down the hall to answer the door. The chatty tone of his voice suggests that he isn't talking to the authorities. She wonders if it will be Artemis with all that wild black hair and energy, just like a puffin, or Zeus, with his bright blue eyes and easily flushed cheeks. She's not sure which one she dreads seeing the most, which one she longs to see the most, as her heart struggles to calm down, her mouth dry like she's eating sawdust.

She hears the front door close and Artemis's loud laughter booming out. Then they are in her space.

"Hey Jesse," says Artemis, perching on the arm of the sofa, wearing ripped jeans and a cotton tee-shirt, her ear studs firmly back in place. "What are you up to?"

She looks so pretty, thinks Jesse, and she's not even trying. Jesse never wears jeans; she prefers looser clothing. Today, she's wearing a floaty white dress covered in hundreds of little red flowers. She's tied her shoulder length light brown hair into a ponytail and she's wearing make-up, just enough to make her feel brave.

"Not much, just watching TV," replies Jesse, feeling her cheeks go red. She wonders if Randy will take Artemis up to his room, since Mum's not here. Where is she?

"Cool. Can we watch with you? How about a film?"

Randy lets out a huge sigh. His luck's not in tonight. Jesse shifts over on the sofa and the three of them sit there, Randy looking at Artemis, Artemis looking at Jesse, Jesse looking at the television.

"I guess I'll get the snacks then!" huffs Randy, disappearing into the kitchen.

While he is gone, Jesse feels Artemis's eyes on her, searching. She smooths down her skirt, wondering if Artemis suspects anything about her. The doorbell rings again and Jesse stands up. *Please don't let it be the police. Don't let Mum be in trouble.*

"Expecting someone?" asks Artemis, one eyebrow raised.

Randy is chatting to someone at the door.

"Look who I found!" he beams, returning to the living room with a bowl of popcorn in his hand.

"Room for one more?" asks Zeus, one eyebrow raised as he looks at Artemis and Jesse on the sofa.

Jesse sits very still and tries to breathe.

"The more the merrier!" trills Artemis, jumping up and leaving a big space next to Jesse, before flopping down on a nearby leather beanbag.

"Artemis," says Randy, still standing in the doorway. "Come on, help me bring some drinks in."

Jesse concentrates on keeping her breathing under control as Zeus sits down next to her.

"You look nice," he says, smiling shyly.

She can't look at him.

"I wondered if… if you wanted to come out with me s-sometime," he stutters.

"I'm home!" calls Ana as she enters the hall.

Upstairs in her bedroom, Jesse breathes a sigh of relief at her mother's return. Sometimes she wishes her mother had a normal job, a normal, safe, predictable, boring job like working in a bank or a supermarket. She stands in front of the mirror, staring at her reflection, her bedroom door locked.

"I am a girl," she says to herself in the mirror.

She pulls her hair out of its ponytail and lets it fall loose to her shoulders.

"I am a girl," she says again, as she wipes her make-up off with cotton wool and baby lotion, staring at herself all the while.

Bare faced, she looks young, like a child. Her skin is pale, her lips thin. Her bright green eyes are the only thing she likes about her face. She hates her strong chin. She closes her eyes and takes a deep breath and she undoes the zip on the back of her dress, letting it fall to the floor, before stepping out of it. It has been a long time since Jesse undressed in front of the mirror, usually dressing with her back turned. But not today. Today, she knows she must face herself.

"I am a girl."

Jesse looks first at her chest, keeping her focus on her white lacy bra. She has well developed breasts for her age, a cleavage to be proud of, especially when some of the girls are still wearing training bras. Debra Simmonds always teases her about her "huge knockers", saying she can always earn a living entertaining rich men if she can't find a decent husband to support her. She unhooks the bra and lets it fall to the floor on top of the dress.

"I am a girl."

Her eyes move down over her toned stomach. She knows some girls would die to have a belly as flat as hers. She thinks of Debra changing for PE with her flabby midriff and flat chest.

"I am a girl."

She forces herself to look at her big pants, the ones she always wears, the ones that fat, middle-aged women wear to hide their lumps and bumps. They do exactly what they say on the packet – keep you smooth. In her big fat control pants, Jesse's body looks almost right.

"I am a girl."

Shaking, she peels off her pants, not moving her eyes. The pants fall to the floor. She removes the strap, her heart pounding as she looks at her naked body from top to toe, taking in her perfect breasts and her penis, knowing what lies underneath. Her breath gets stuck in her throat, her eyes fill.

"I AM a girl," she says again.

3

"I want to have the operation," Jesse blurts out to her mother's back the next morning, as Ana reaches up to get crockery out of the cupboard.

There is a moment's silence, punctuated by the clatter of dishes as Ana put them down on the worktop. Jesse hears Randy walking about upstairs in his room, no doubt exhausted after a late night with Artemis.

"Darling, that's wonderful!" says Ana, spinning round to face Jesse and pulling her towards her. "Are you sure you're ready? You know I don't want you to feel pressurised just because Randy went ahead at your age."

"I need to have it," says Jesse quietly. "It's time."

"Well if you're sure, I'll start to get the ball rolling for the arrangements. We'll do it after your exams. Not long to go now until you break up for summer."

"Thank you," says Jesse, busying herself with laying the table. "Oh and Mum? Are you in any trouble, you know, with your work?"

"No trouble, darling," says Ana, with a tight smile. "Everything will be okay. Don't you worry about a thing."

Randy thumps down the stairs, grabs a slice of toast, moaning about a headache and disappears back upstairs, leaving Jesse and Ana to eat together in peace. Jesse can think of nothing else to say to her mother, the announcement has drained her of words and emotion. She feels as empty as the cereal packet that sits on the table. She eats her muesli and concentrates on each grain. Ana watches her as they eat, sitting in a kitchen like mother and daughter. Mother and daughter-to-be.

"Oh and Jesse," says her mother, watching Jesse scrape her bowl clean. "If it makes it any easier, I do think you're doing the right thing. It's good to get things finalised before you turn sixteen. As long as you are totally sure that you feel ready to transform into a young woman."

"I'm ready," whispers Jesse, her face set.

Once Jesse has left the room, Ana collapses back into the chair.

Ana is fifteen, hanging out of her bedroom window, long, blonde hair billowing, as she looks down at the garden, set for her brother, George's eleventh birthday. It hasn't changed that much since he was born. There's a patio where the weeds used to be and the old slide and sand pit have long been taken down and given away but the apple tree still drops rotten fruit over the lawn every summer, sticking to the soles of Ana's sandals and attracting the wasps. They have put a big table under the shade of the tree and covered it with a checked red and white table cloth. It is packed with crisps and sandwiches with food wrap still on them to keep the flies away, George's favourite Swiss roll and jugs of fruit punch.

The weather is not as fine as they had hoped, a little choppy for a party, the edges of the table cloth whipping up into the air. The breeze blows through her ears, the wind chimes rattle in the trees, making her think of the triangle and tambourine that George still loves to play.

She pulls her head back inside the room.

Her mother is screaming.

Jesse has lunch with Artemis most days at school now. Artemis is fun and it's better than sitting on your own every day. They have been shopping at the mall together at the weekend too, much to Randy's annoyance. He hates them spending time together, hates the way they gossip together, leaving him out.

"So when are you actually going to go out with Zeus?" asks Artemis over lunch, talking with her mouth full.

"You're so gross!" laughs Jesse. "Do I really need to see your mushed up spring roll?"

"Sorry," she laughs, closing her mouth and swallowing. "Now stop avoiding the question. He asked you out, what, at least a fortnight ago. So what's happening?"

"I told him I need to wait until the summer holidays. I want to get through my exams and stuff first," says Jesse, not quite meeting Artemis's eye.

"Oh, come on. You can still go on one little date at the weekend! Are you sure that's all it is?" she asks, her face suddenly serious.

"I would have still gone out with Randy before he had the op, you know. I would have been his girlfriend even if he wasn't a he."

Jesse puts down her knife and fork.

"You know about Randy's op?" whispers Jesse. "You know about me?"

"Yeah, I don't see the big deal."

Jesse's head is spinning. She is so mad at Randy for telling her their secret. He had no right to tell anybody about her. Their mother could get arrested. Other students walk past, chattering, pushing, bags swinging.

"So, so, you can't tell him! He'll think I'm a freak! He won't want to go out with me any more!" says Jesse, standing up and pushing the table back.

"Shh, sit back down, stupid," says Artemis, putting her hand on Jesse's. "I'm not going to tell him. I just wanted you to know that I know. You're not the only ones, Jesse. And not everyone has it done either. You don't have to. If you don't want to."

"What do you mean?" asks Jesse, as Artemis's words

rush round in her brain, making her head hurt. "But you…?"

"Yeah, I'm a hundred per cent girl." Artemis laughs. "Had the snip at birth. I still have to go for the doctor's appointments and all that, of course. But sometimes I wonder…"

Jesse waits for the words to follow but they remain silent, like George's ghost.

"I want you to meet my friends Ork and Max," says Artemis, out of the blue. "I can take you to meet them on Friday."

Jesse stares at Artemis.

"Promise me you'll meet Ork and Max," persists Artemis, her pupils wide and black.

4

There were lots of other families in the communal house. Jesse remembers a lot of green and brown. There was a huge forest at the back of the house, an enchanted forest full of magic, of the unicorns and fairies and elves from the stories the mothers used to read to them. But it wasn't just the bark and leaves and grass. Other things were green and brown too. Babies wrapped in khaki-coloured blankets, toddlers in chocolate brown pyjamas, bedroom walls painted lime, wooden floorboards, modelling clay and paints in natural shades.

When she closes her eyes, Jesse can travel back to her three-year-old self, her first conscious memory, the first day she remembers being alive. She cannot remember anything about being born or being a baby. The only things she knows about herself before she turned three are things her mother has told her. Second hand scenes. Imaginings. A picture of herself being born out in the forest with the other mothers holding Ana's shoulders and singing lullabies. The sound of her first cry, as pure as birdsong, as angry as a wolf. These are the things Ana has told her. But the image of herself at three is as real as the image of herself right now, lying in her bed under her cotton sheet in her long white nightdress.

There are lots of children playing in the room, running, toddling, sitting. They have long hair in different colours: blonde, auburn, brown and black, skin, which is white or pink or pale gold or brown. But their clothes are the same colour. A nothing colour. Khaki. Mummies sit amongst the children, talking, laughing, interacting. A child with red hair and freckles is rolling a ball towards her.

"Catch!"

Jesse stares at the ball knocking against her bare toes in their open sandals.

"Catch!" says the other child again, running to get the ball and placing it in Jesse's hands. "Look!"

As the child's hand moves forwards to push the ball into her, the skin of her wrist pushes out of its khaki sleeve, revealing a bracelet, which startles Jesse. She has seen jewellery before. Her mother wears a silver locket and a bracelet with an emerald stone. But this child's bracelet is different from any she has seen. It is a colour she hasn't seen before. Jesse doesn't know the word for the colour.

Later she tells her mother she wants a bracelet like the one she has seen. Ana asks her to show her the bracelet. Jesse runs over to the child and pulls her sleeve up, making her cry. Ana stares at it and says she can't have a bracelet like that but they will make a lovely bracelet out of feather or twigs or leaves. Soon after, the child with the red hair and freckles and her mother leave the community. Jesse doesn't see the colour pink again until they move out when she is eight.

"What's up with you?" Jesse asks her brother on Thursday evening after dinner. "It's all right for you. You've finished all your exams, you should be celebrating!"

"Well I'm not." Randy, taps his fingers of his right hand on the knee of his jeans, and randomly presses buttons on the TV remote with the other. "I'm bored! So I've done my exams and if I'm good enough I'll go to university and if not, I'll go to vocational tech and then what? I'll get a job and get married and maybe have kids and it will all start again. It's so totally boring!"

Jesse isn't in the mood for her brother's melodramatics, not tonight. Tonight she is thinking about Artemis. She is thinking about what Artemis said the last time they spoke. She is trying to imagine Artemis as a boy but she can't because Artemis is nothing like a boy. She is curvy and soft and gentle and smiley and her skin is soft and smooth. Jesse looks at her own arm resting on the sofa, at the dark hairs that litter her pale skin. No, Artemis's parents definitely did the right thing with her. She is thinking about the fact that she is supposed to be meeting Artemis's friend, Ork, tomorrow after school. The fact that she didn't promise but she didn't say no either and that as she stared blankly at Artemis, Artemis talked and talked about Ork but really said nothing at all. She realises that she doesn't know the first thing about this Ork person, not even if Ork is a boy or a girl. Maybe it will be someone like Uncle George, who was turned into a boy when she should have been a girl and that was why Artemis wants Jesse to meet him, as a warning not to go ahead with the operation. But Ork isn't dead like Uncle George. Maybe Ork was assigned the wrong gender too but it was fixed before it was too late. Maybe he was made into a boy and then made back into a girl. Jesse's head hurts. She wants to fast forward the next twenty-four hours and find out who Ork is. But before she can do that, she will have to suffer Mrs Pritchard's lesson tomorrow.

"Did you speak to Artemis today?" asks Randy, no longer pressing the remote control.

"No, I haven't seen her since yesterday. Why?"

"No reason," says Randy, standing up.

"Have you two had a fight or something?" asks Jesse.

Her brother doesn't normally act this weird.

"Shut up and mind your own business! Do I keep asking you whether you've snogged Zeus yet?"

"I didn't…"

Randy storms out of the room and up to his bedroom.

Jesse hears the slam of his door. She wonders what is going on with him and Artemis. Well, they've definitely snogged, that's for sure. She's seen Artemis coming out of Randy's room with stubble rash all over her chin. She guesses they've done a lot more but she's not about to ask Artemis how far she's gone with her brother, is she? That would be way too gross. She pushes the image of Randy and Artemis out of her mind. Instead she sees Randy, aged four, in the commune with her, running around in his khaki uniform, his brown hair long and his knees dirty, before he was a boy.

"God created men and women as different but equal members of society. Discuss."

Mrs Pritchard is standing at the front of the class. She wears a starchy, black jacket and a tartan skirt. Her body is like a box, all hard straight edges, thick and chunky. She never smiles.

"Debra," she fires.

All eyes turn to look at Debra.

"Would you please stand up and read us your essay?"

Mrs Pritchard likes to do this every time they have homework, make people read out their essay before anyone knows what marks they have been awarded. So you never know whether you have been asked to present your work as an example of excellence for others to follow or to be ridiculed and told why you have done it all wrong.

Debra stands up nervously. She looks around the class at the other girls. Jesse looks down at her own essay, as though trying to find clues about its worth. Debra coughs and then begins.

"God created man and woman in the image of God (Genesis. 1:24-31). Humankind is made of men and women. Sin entered the world because of the fall of man (Genesis. 3:16). We must stamp out rebellion against God's order."

She pauses and looks up at Mrs Pritchard.

"Go on," she urges, not giving anything away.

"Woman was created as an equal to man and as his helper. The woman must submit to the man in accordance with the authority which God created just like Christ submitted to his Father and the Spirit to the Son and the Father in the Trinity…"

Jesse wonders why she wants to be a woman if what Debra is saying is true. She zones out and thinks about meeting Ork after school.

5

"Where are we going?" Jesse asks Artemis as she leads her in the opposite direction from home.

Pink cherry blossom falls from the trees that line the street. The little floating pink petals make Jesse think for a moment of the bracelet and the commune.

"We're going to meet Ork and Max!" beams Artemis, her eyes glittering, her step quickening as she pulls Jesse along.

"Yes, but where? In their house? Are they boys? Are they brothers or friends or what? Why won't you tell me anything?"

Artemis laughs and tosses back her hair. "You'll find out about that crowd soon enough."

"That crowd?" says Jesse, suddenly nervous. "I thought we were just meeting Ork and Max. Who else are we meeting?"

"Stop worrying. It'll be fine. Prepare to be enlightened."

Artemis is practically skipping now.

"I am worried," says Jesse. "I don't even know these people. Has Randy met them? Are you guys okay?"

Artemis's smile falls at the mention of Randy's name.

"Have you had an argument? Hey, this isn't some kind of blind date, is it? A foursome? You're supposed to be going out with my brother!"

"It's not a date!" laughs Artemis. "Me and Randy, well, I don't want to be rude but I don't really want to talk about it."

Jesse looks at Artemis. "Sorry, I didn't mean to pry."

"It's okay. You're not. Look, the thing is…" Artemis stops walking for a moment and turns to face Jesse. "Randy hasn't met Ork or Max. I don't think he'd understand so it might be better if you didn't say anything."

"Oh, okay. No worries. You know, Randy is quite open-minded. Don't forget he didn't have Assignment until last year. He knows a lot."

Jesse wonders exactly how much Artemis knows about their mother, about how they were raised.

"Yeah, well, he doesn't know about this," says Artemis, starting to walk again, a serious look on her face. "Did you bring your stuff to get changed into? We'll change in a minute."

Jesse taps her bag. "Why can't we just keep our school uniform on anyway?"

"They're older than us. They don't go to school."

"How old?"

"Eighteen."

"So what's the big deal. They know we're only fifteen and go to school, right? You've not pretended we're older or anything crazy like that, have you?"

"No, no, I haven't told any crazy lies," says Artemis, rolling her eyes. "You don't get it. They've *never* been to school. We don't want to stand out as different."

"Oh. Who are these people? I'm scared now," says Jesse.

"Don't worry, most of them are all right."

This does nothing to reassure Jesse. Artemis pulls her round a sharp corner where the houses fall away and the street becomes darker. At Artemis's insistence, they change in an alleyway. Jesse hates changing in public. On PE days, she puts her thick navy sports knickers over her big pants before she leaves home in the morning, and pulls her PE skirt on under her kilt. She turns away from Artemis and tries to change in a similarly surreptitious manner. Artemis told her it might be best to wear trousers not a skirt. The only trousers she has are a pair of loose fitting black cargo pants, which Artemis says are okay. She wears them with a loose red tee-shirt, her uniform stuffed back inside her bag. Artemis flicks on a torch and hands it to Jesse, before getting another one out of her bag.

"Just in case," she says, shrugging.

"In case what?" asks Jesse, eyes wide.

"You are so easy to wind up!" laughs Artemis. "It's just a bit dark and gloomy round here. I thought you'd feel better with one of these." She shakes the torch.

"Yeah, well I don't," humphs Jesse. "How do you know Ork and Max anyway? Where did you meet them? Are they from your dance class or drama or one of your other extra-curricular clubs?"

"No, no, nothing like that," laughs Artemis. "I met Max a couple of years ago in the park and we hit it off straight away. Such a lovely, warm, genuine person. You'll love Max. I didn't know anything about their world but Max introduced me to Ork and I sort of ended up hanging out with them sometimes, even though I'm not one of them or anything. Max is very accepting but they're not all like that…"

"I've no idea what you're talking about," says Jesse, "and I'm not sure I want to."

They fall into silent strides together, walking until Jesse can feel blisters forming on the back of her heels, past the old industrial estate, past the wasteland, into nothingness. Just when she thinks she can walk no longer Artemis says, "We're here."

Jesse looks around. She has no idea where they are. She has never been this way. In fact, she has never been very far at all without her mother, although Ana, Randy and Jesse have moved about the country many times from east to west and south to north. They have travelled far and wide together moving home and meeting with people from the commune, Ana's friends. Jesse used to love being in her mother's car as a child, setting off on a long journey with a packet of sandwiches and a flask of hot chocolate, board games and colouring books to keep them entertained. She never used to think about the destination when she was a child and living in the moment as only children can. She used to see each new move as an adventure, where she got to explore the nooks and crannies of another place, claim her new bedroom and set about making it hers. It didn't matter if it was a poky old flat on a sink estate, with no garden. She didn't even mind when they lived above the greengrocers, the stench of rotten fruit drifting up through the windows. But now she felt differently about a lot of things.

"Come on," says Artemis. "It's this way."

Artemis leads her through more alleyways until they reach a metal staircase. The stink of the overflowing bins beneath it takes Jesse's breath away. She feels damp heat on her back. Her cargo pants are sticking to her thighs. Tentatively, Jesse follows Artemis up the staircase, tensing with the creek of each step, trying not to touch the rusty handrail.

"Wait here a minute while I find Ork," says Artemis.

Jesse stands at the top of what she guesses is a fire escape, her heart pounding in her chest as Artemis disappears into the building, releasing a wave of heat and noise as the door swings open and closed again. As she stands there she wonders what on earth persuaded her to come to this creepy place, to meet some random people she knows nothing about. Five minutes later the door opens and Jesse hopes that Artemis hasn't found Ork and that they can run home together, back to the safety of her nice, comfy family home with Randy, who might irritate her with his moaning and teasing but is really an okay brother, and her mother, who she knows has only ever wanted what's best for both her children.

But it isn't Artemis.

"Oh! You gave me a fright! I didn't think anyone was here!" says the person standing two inches away from Jesse.

Jesse can't help but stare at the girl, at her hair, completely shaved on one side and long and red on the other, the rows of earrings and facial piercings, the tattoo of a snake on the girl's slender neck. She must be a girl because she is wearing a bright pink tee-shirt, revealing two small mounds on her chest. Her top is emblazoned with the word 'One'. Her arms are muscular, her nails bitten down. She feels something shift in her memory as she looks at this girl.

"S-sorry," stammers Jesse, "I'm waiting for my friend."

"Who's your friend?"

"Artemis. I don't know if you know her. She's friends with Ork and Max."

"Oh, I know her all right," says the girl, observing Jesse through partly closed eyes. "So who are you?"

"I'm Jesse. I, I'm supposed to be meeting them.'

The girl smiles. "Oh, I know who you are."

Jesse stares blankly at the girl.

"You'll like Ork," she says. "Everyone does. So what are you then?"

Jesse doesn't know how to answer the question. It starts spitting with rain and she wants to be inside but at the same time she wants to run as far away as she can get, through pouring rain, thunder and lightning.

The door opens again and Artemis stands there grinning.

"Come in out of the rain, Jesse! Ork wants to meet you!" she says before her eyes flick to the smoking girl.

A look passes between them, a look that Jesse can't fathom. Artemis pulls her inside into a huge room, a hall. It is vibrant, full of noise and heat and colour, full of people, some moving about, playing pool or messing about, some sitting on big multi-coloured bean bags chatting, just like at the youth club. Her eyes scan the room. There must be about fifty people in here, thinks Jesse. But it isn't like the youth club. At the youth club, you see girls like Debra, free of the drab uniform, dressed up in spangles and shimmer, hair highlighted and carefully curled or straightened, wearing make-up that looks too old for her, leaning conspiratorially into her friend, Louisa, whispering about boys and laughing, looking at their immaculately manicured nails. You see boys like Zeus, always on the move, under the radar, in scuffed trainers, who sit with their legs open, slouching and looking like they'd rather be somewhere else. It isn't like the commune either, where another drab uniform ruled. No, here there is an explosion of difference but sameness.

"Hi, I'm Ork. Artemis has told me a lot about you."

The words come from a boy, or is it a girl, with short dark hair, blue eyes rimmed with black kohl pencil, full lips and very pale skin. The boy-girl wears faded skinny jeans and a black shirt with a tasselled multi-coloured scarf wrapped around his neck covering his chest. Jesse stops herself from looking at the crotch for evidence.

"She hasn't told me much about you!" says Jesse, giggling with nerves.

"Then you'll just have to get to know me for yourself," says Ork, a slow smile starting.

6

The young woman has lank, greasy hair and is short and thin, wearing a baggy grey rain coat. An older woman welcomes her into the room and offers her a seat.

"Welcome, dear. My name's Ana."

The door clicks quietly closed behind them. Soft classical music emanates from a small battered silver portable music player on the desk. The room is stuffy, the battered wooden windows painted closed. The interior is shabby, with peeling paint on the walls and a worn rug on the floor. The scent of burning incense fills the young woman's nostrils. She closes her eyes for a moment, as tears prick at the corners.

"Would you like anything to drink?" asks Ana, gesturing to the makeshift refreshment corner, a kettle and tray with plastic cups balanced on a wooden crate. "Some water or juice? Or perhaps a herbal tea?"

The young woman, still standing, shakes her head, with terror in her eyes as they dart around the room.

"Don't be afraid," says Ana gently. "We are here to help you. Please, sit down."

The woman takes off her coat, revealing the bump protruding from her belly. She sits down on the chair, on the drape embroidered with elephants and doves. She wrings her hands and her cheap black and white plastic bangles clang against one another.

"Now, let me see," says Ana, tucking her hair behind her ears and looking at the pages of her blue suede notebook. "It was Joyce who found you and talked to you about what we do, wasn't it?"

The woman nods.

"Do you have any questions at this stage?"

"I'm not sure," says the woman in a tiny voice, tears falling.

"It's okay. We have plenty of time," reassures Ana. "Let me go through a few things with you."

The woman nods and puts a protective hand over her baby bump.

"At Natural Souls we believe that every human soul has a predetermined gender. As you will know, due to humankind's abuse of nature and exposure to agricultural pesticides and other chemicals, we have witnessed many generations of babies without clear physical gender characteristics. At first it was just the fish and polar bears. No-one thought it would happen to us. They thought humans were above nature. But they were wrong."

The woman is now rubbing her belly, making the bangles jiggle together some more.

Ana tugs at the locket she wears with George's picture inside.

"The majority of babies are now born biologically inter-sex, with a combination of ovarian and testicular tissue and XX and XY chromosomes and ambiguous external genitalia. The government has outlawed a liberal response citing ridiculous fears about the breakdown in moral and family values. Their solution to this is to force Compulsory Gender Assignment on all intersex babies at birth depending on assessment of external genitalia and with a little help from their quotas but we do not believe this is an appropriate or compassionate solution to a man-made problem."

The woman hangs her head down and starts to cry.

"It's okay, dear. I know this happened to you. How do you feel about being assigned as female?" Ana leans forward and hands the young woman a tissue.

The woman cries hard into the tissue and blows her nose before composing herself and beginning to talk. "It's not that. I'm okay with what happened to me but I've known people who weren't."

She pauses and Ana nods, not taking her eyes off the woman's face.

"I think we have all known people who were assigned the wrong gender," she says gently. "Sometimes, the person keeps their pain locked inside so it is difficult for others to see whereas other people act in a way that leaves no doubt about the horror they have lived through but the consequences are always tragic."

"I'm just so confused about what to do for the baby," blurts out the woman, starting to cry again. "I believe what you are all saying at Natural Souls. I don't want them to make my baby a boy if she is supposed to be a girl or vice versa but I don't want to raise her as a freak either!"

"It's okay, they won't be a freak," says Ana, reaching out to put her hand on the woman's hand. "Many women have raised their babies gender neutral until the children have found their true gender identity. This practice has been going on underground for many, many years. Natural Souls conducted some research to find out how practices have changed over the years and I discovered that in my grandparents' time when only a quarter of babies were affected, things were in some ways easier. There was less legislation for a start. The Gender Assignment Act had not been passed and that made all the difference. People were left to get on with things in their own way. Of course, everything was hushed up and swept under the carpet but parents didn't have to worry about the law in the way we all do now. Everything has got harder, society is harsher." Ana shakes her head and smiles sadly. "But your baby will be just fine if you give them the time they need to find their own path. I raised my own children that way and they are just fine."

The woman stares into Ana's eyes, full of hope.

"Did you? And they are okay? They chose the right path and they are happy?"

"Well," says Ana shifting back in her seat, "my son, Randy, discovered at age seven that he was meant to be a boy. Jesse took a little longer, but when she was nine, she wanted to be known as a girl. That's when we left the commune and moved into the community, starting both at school, with the false ID, and they were introduced to their new school friends as brother and sister. Randy had his operation last year, aged fifteen and Jesse is going to have hers over the summer, now she is fifteen too. So yes, I think they chose the right path. Jesse is a little scared right now, understandably, as you are right now too. But they had time to decide and that is what we want for your little boy or girl too. Now that I've told you the names of my children, will you tell me what your name is and how old you are?"

"It's Julie. I'm, I'm seventeen." Her shoulders relax and she smiles tentatively.

"Thank you, Julie," says Ana returning the smile. "Trust is very important here. Do you feel you can trust me and talk openly?"

"Yes," replies Julie, her hands now still in her lap, the bangles silent.

"Then I want you to tell me how you are feeling right now."

"I'm scared… I was at home with my mum when that thing came on the news about the couple that got arrested for being part of the Natural Baby Movement."

A frown passes across Ana's face. "That was very unfortunate."

"Plus, I heard that the government is outlawing unisex names, so I don't know what name to give the baby."

"That problem is not insurmountable," says Ana gently. "You can live in one of the communes with the baby until the gender becomes clear. Certificates can be… arranged later. We'll protect you and the baby."

"I worry the baby will go to hell," says Julie in a clear, crisp voice.

Ana breathes in sharply.

"Mum didn't know I was pregnant. I was still able to hide it then. But she said those people would go to hell for going against God and so would the babies because they would be freaks of nature."

"Julie, I understand it is very scary when someone says something like that to you but you have to understand that these comments are made out of fear and ignorance. Ninety-one per cent of babies born now are freaks of nature. It's just that mankind now tries to obliterate that fact by forcing surgery and other inhumane procedures on innocent non-consenting children. We do not make children in God's image by operating on at birth. We do not make them holy. We go against God when we do not take the time required to discover God's intention for each child. Do you understand?"

"Yes. If you can promise me that my baby won't go to hell then I want to join."

"I promise," says Ana, smiling.

7

"Does it hurt?" Jesse asks Randy, as they sit in the garden, enjoying the hot afternoon.

The flowers are out in full, glorious bloom, the garden a feast of diverse colours, textures, shapes and aromas. Ana has worked hard in the little garden of their ground floor maisonette and her work has paid off. Jesse fingers the magnificent silver foliage of the artemisias, waiting for Randy's answer, before reaching over and pulling one of his earphones out.

"What?" replies Randy irritably, lying back on the wooden sunlounger, eyes closed.

"Does the operation hurt?" Jesse sits forward staring expectantly at Randy.

Today, she is wearing baggy red shorts and a flowery top. She likes red. It is almost pink but braver.

"I dunno, do I? I was asleep when they did it to me. I'm sure it would hurt if you were awake!" Randy turns his face towards Jesse but keeps his sunglasses on and the other earphone firmly in place.

"But I mean afterwards. Is it really, really sore down there?"

Randy shrugs. "It's not great but you don't mind because it's a great thing to finally be a boy, or in your case a stupid girl."

He turns his head away and stuffs his other earphone back in, nodding his head to the beat of the music.

"But... please Randy..." She holds onto his arm until he takes the earphone back out again.

"What?!"

"You know, is it okay afterwards?"

"You really should be asking a girl all this stuff," he moans. "It'll be easier for you, I reckon."

"Will it?" she asks, wondering if it's true.

It's so hard to get any information on this stuff. There is nowhere official to turn, nobody to talk to, nothing to read. You can't just pop along to your family doctor for an open discussion. Neither Jesse or Randy are registered with a medical doctor anyway. They see Maya for treatments when they get ill. She gives them herbs and teas and acupuncture.

"Yeah, you just snip a few bits off and away you go!" he smirks. "You haven't got to have your whole insides ripped out."

"Is it awful?" she asks, biting her lip. "Does it work properly? Does it feel all right once it's all healed?"

"Jesse!" shouts Randy, "I really do not want to be discussing my sex life with my sister! I thought you were going to see Maya again. I thought Mum was arranging for you to talk to some girls who'd been through it?"

"Yeah, I know. I've already spoken to two girls."

"And?"

"And I don't know."

Jesse hadn't really got to know Ork at all that night. Artemis got some drinks for them and then disappeared, leaving the two of them talking, sitting opposite each other on bean bags. Ork had spoken to her for over an hour, asking her loads of questions about herself. Just simple things – her favourite bands, what she likes to do, what she's studying, what she wants to do with her life. She found herself blushing at the attention. The way he asked questions and leant back somehow leaving her a big space to fill meant she had spoken about herself more than she usually would. Still, she didn't know what she wanted to do with her life. She couldn't imagine committing herself to a cause like her mother but she couldn't see herself sliding into one of the careers expected of girls either, the things they spoke about at school – nursing, caring, looking after people, beauty, hairdressing, making other girls look the way they were supposed to. Ork seemed really interested in getting to know her but she left feeling she knew hardly anything about him. She knew he was home schooled and that he liked to grow things – herbs, fruit, vegetables, flowers – and that he doesn't live with his parents any more. That was all. She thinks of Ork as him, although he isn't really a him or her. He's like her. Except he hasn't chosen. That was the big thing she found out about him and the others. None of the people there that night has chosen. That's what Ork told her. Jesse can't imagine still not knowing when you are sixteen. Her mother seems pretty certain that everyone would know by then.

After all the talk about music and art and exams, when she was relaxed and starting to enjoy herself, he says, "So, Artemis tells me you haven't had Assignment either?"

She nods. The fact that he's told her that none of the people here have even chosen yet makes Jesse feel more comfortable with him knowing that she hasn't had Assignment. It isn't like at school where everyone was assigned at birth and would think you were a freak for not having been assigned. And anyway, she's having it all sorted out next month.

"But you are going to have it done?"

"Well, yeah," she says, shrugging. "My brother had it last year before he started going out with Artemis. My turn now!"

Ork looks down at the floor like he wants to say something but doesn't want to at the same time. Then he looks up again and smiles. "I'm guessing you've chosen to be a girl then?"

Hearing those words coming out of Ork's mouth makes her feel strange, like Zeus makes her feel, but kind of different.

"Well, do I look like a boy?" she laughs, feeling nervous, then wondering if she's said the wrong thing. Nobody here looks like a boy or a girl. They are all androgynous in appearance.

"I thought I recognised the girl with the pink tee-shirt and the red hair," adds Jesse, still trying to remember where she might have seen her before.

"Max isn't a girl, okay?" said Ork, looking serious.

"Max?" The name takes her back to the day at the commune, where the child with red hair and freckles and the pink bracelet is rolling a ball towards her.

"Yeah, you look like you've seen a ghost."

"It's just I think I used to know her, I mean… What do you call people then if you don't call them him or her?"

"What did you call people at the commune?" asks Ork, one eyebrow raised.

Jesse wonders how Ork knew she lived in a commune when she was younger. She supposes Randy told Artemis. He seems to have told her everything else.

"We called them a person. We said 'they' and 'them'."

"Well, that's a start," says Ork. "But we prefer different pronouns here. 'They' and 'them' are plural. We are all individuals. We say no to masculine and feminine pronouns. We say 'p-h-e', that's pronounced 'phe' instead of 'he' and 'she', 'p-h-e-r-m' pronounced 'pherm' instead of him and her, and 'p-h-e-r-s' or 'phers' instead of his and hers. Do you think you could use those terms when you are with us?"

"Sure," says Jesse, feeling she shouldn't be here.

Jesse thinks about the two girls who were sent to talk to her, driven to the maisonette by Maya in her clapped out, old, white Beetle one afternoon when Ana was out at meetings: Jo, now fifteen, who'd had Assignment aged twelve and Ash, eighteen, who'd had Assignment at fifteen, the same age as Jesse. Maya arrived with a bunch of pink carnations, still in their plastic wrap. Jesse knew it was meant as an icebreaker, a gift to make her feel at ease. But she also knew that her mother would hate the sight of them when she came home and saw the too bright flowers and everything they stood for, displayed unashamedly in the glass jug that normally contained orange juice. Sometimes, Maya doesn't think.

"Darling," she'd said, kissing Jesse on both cheeks as she handed over the gift and swished her green, pink and blue striped scarf around her neck.

Maya had introduced them and then left the girls to talk, sitting round Ana's old oak table.

Jo, six foot tall and nonetheless wearing black shiny patent high heels, towered over Jesse, strong and imposing in a tight black mini dress revealing acres of fake-tanned flesh, her long, shiny hair, dyed a vibrant auburn, her fingers covered in glittery rings. When she spoke, in her loud, brash voice, Jesse had to stop herself from staring at the girl's eyebrows, which were completely painted on in auburn pencil, no hint of any hair on her face or body. You could tell just by looking that she'd had a lot of cosmetic surgery, her expressionless face was disarming.

"My last surgery was breast enlargement and I had a couple of ribs removed to make my waist smaller," Jo replied casually when Jesse asked her about her surgery.

"I meant the Gender Assignment," said Jesse. "What was the procedure really like?"

"You shouldn't believe everything people tell you," said Jo. "It's not that bad, especially if you get a top surgeon. Are you having Tom Donald Browne? He's the best, you know. And very discreet."

Jesse hadn't particularly noticed Ash at that point, her eyes drawn to Jo and her striking looks. Ash sat beside her, now softly tapping her glass. She was petite, drowning in a grey cotton smock worn over baggy jeans. Jesse turned her attention to the older girl. She wore wire rimmed glasses and her pale face was devoid of make-up, her frown clearly discernible under bushy eyebrows.

When Ash finally spoke, she said, "What you are about to do is a very big deal, and there's absolutely no point in pretending otherwise. Oh, and I wouldn't go to Browne. I've heard bad things about him."

Jo and Ash scowled at one another.

8

There is plenty of advice in girlie magazines about how you are supposed to be on a date – how to dress, how to act, what to say. Ask Alex is Jesse's favourite agony column, even if it never features anyone like her. She likes the fact that Alex is a unisex name. Alexandra or Alexander? Whenever she comes across a person with an ambiguous name, she can't help but wonder. But her mother always knows who's had Assignment and who hasn't; she is very well connected in the underworld. Looking at the two centimetre square head shot of Alex on the page leaves no questions about her gender. She's all hair clips and lip gloss. The big sister Jesse doesn't have.

Zeus asked her to go to his friend Justin's party with him. Artemis is going with Randy and Debra is going with some skinny boy called Derek who makes her look fat. She's been moaning about it to all the girls at school. Debra likes Derek; she thinks their names go well together; she has been writing 'Debra heart Derek' all over her exercise book with her fancy pencil with the smelly strawberry shaped rubber at the end. Even though she likes Derek, she doesn't like looking fat. She will have to wear black; it will make her look slimmer. She's asked Derek to wear something pale to bulk him out a bit.

Jesse sits on the edge of her bed, scanning the well-worn page again, hoping to find more answers, more inspiration.

Dear Alex, I'm going on my first date and I really want him to like me. What should I do? Yours anxiously, K x

Dear K, just be yourself and you'll be fine. It doesn't hurt to make a bit of an effort with your appearance

Jesse looks over at her reflection in the mirror. In her duck egg blue dress, she feels neither comfortable nor a little bit special. She takes off the abhorrent garment and chucks it on the bed, raking through her wardrobe in her bra and big knickers. She wonders at a pair of pistachio wide leg linen pants before shuddering. Not green! Not blue! She wishes she had something pink right now, or sparkly. But the nearest colour she has in her wardrobe is red. She fishes out a red cotton top and puts it on with baggy jeans. It looks gross. She cannot believe that she ever thought she looked good in red. Red is not brave. Red is violent. Stripping down to her underwear again, she glances back at her reflection and wonders what Ork looks like naked. Does he look like her? Under his scarf and baggy tee-shirt, she couldn't tell whether he had breasts. Maybe he wears them strapped down or maybe he doesn't have any. She tries to push the image of the nude Ork out of her mind and think about Zeus instead.

Zeus is all boy with his muscular shoulders and thick chunky thighs. Her jaw looks feminine in comparison to his, her body soft. This is exactly what she needs right now. A date with Zeus. So what if she hasn't had the operation yet? She's not planning to get that close for at least a good few months and she'll be healed by then. Anyway, she'll be going to stay with Maya out in the sticks somewhere soon enough so she won't be seeing anyone for a while. She needs this date with Zeus tonight to make her feel like a girl and to make sure that he's into her, that he won't go off with anyone else while she's away 'on holiday'. She wishes she could leave the country and go somewhere far away, hot and tropical, like the places she had read about in her mother's old, paperback romance novels, the well-thumbed pages transporting her to new and exciting worlds. But she knows that is not possible. Residents are not allowed out of the country unless on official business of work permits. Jesse finds a multi-coloured patterned dress at the back of her wardrobe, one she hasn't worn for ages. Patterns are good. You can hide things in patterns. She adds make-up and curls and shoes with just a bit of a heel.

"Whoa, what happened in here?" exclaims Artemis as she walks into Jesse's bedroom thirty minutes later.

By the time Artemis arrives, Jesse is no longer sure about the patterned dress. Surely yellow and purple clash? Together they look like vomit. Artemis waltzes into Jesse's bedroom in a waft of perfume, smelling just like the flowers that Ana planted in the garden last year. She is wearing tight black jeans with sandals, a white silk top and silver jewellery, her long hair loose and straight. She looks pure and smooth, whereas Jesse feels complicated and jagged.

"You look great," says Artemis, steering Jesse out of the bedroom when she says she might change into something else. "Very glamorous."

Jesse doesn't want to look glamorous. This definitely means she looks like someone who has tried too hard. Glamour is not natural beauty. Glamour is seedy and tacky, strippers and pole dancers. She thinks about Debra's comments about her entertaining rich men and she feels suddenly sick.

"I might have to go back. I'm not feeling too good," she says at the end of the road. "I feel sick. Maybe I have a bug or ate something dodgy."

"Oh no you don't," laughs Artemis, flicking her hair out of her face. "Sick with first date nerves is all. Once we get there, you'll be fine."

Jesse is not sure. She has practised slow dancing with Artemis in the bedroom, using her arms in a way that gives her a little body space. She has made Artemis swear that she can't feel any bulges where they shouldn't be.

When they get there, the place is already heaving. Artemis leads Jesse by the hand through the house to the crowded kitchen looking for Randy and Zeus who made their way over straight from football practice. Artemis says hello to Justin, who nods at Jesse. His thin, mousy hair is plastered to his sweaty forehead. He smiles inanely and shrugs his shoulders, apparently unbothered by the number of people streaming through the door. His parents have gone out, he says. They won't be back until at least two o'clock. It is only eight o'clock now. They have six hours of fun ahead of them. Jesse knows she cannot stay until two o'clock. Her mother is coming to pick her up at midnight. She is Cinderella without the glittery ball gown. They pass Debra and Derek arguing by the downstairs toilet. Artemis is staring at Debra who is wearing a very flattering black halter neck dress with a wide belt that makes her look as though she has an hourglass figure. Jesse hates her multi-coloured, patterned dress. She is a jigsaw puzzle covered in sick.

"There they are!" says Artemis, jumping up and down as she spots the boys through the window in the garden. "Randy!"

Zeus turns to look at the doorway. He seems bigger than Jesse remembered, huge like a giant, his limbs like tree trunks. He strides towards the girls with a serious look on his face. The air seems to part for him. Wind blows across the garden making the leaves fall and grass bend. He is sky and thunder. Jesse shivers.

"Hi Jesse," he says, taking her hand.

They go inside, leaving Artemis and Randy out in the garden, Jesse feeling grateful for the loud music. They stand too close to the speakers sipping Justin's homemade punch listening to the tracks change. One sip makes Jesse feel funny. The bass reverberates through her whole body, electrifying her. Zeus stares at her as though he is trying to work something out. She feels panic and drinks more punch until the feeling subsides. As Zeus goes to refill their glasses, she sees Debra and Derek up against the wall, Derek's hand squeezing Debra all over. Debra's eyeliner has smudged, her lipstick has disappeared, her head rolls back and Derek kisses her neck. Jesse feels like she might faint. She looks away.

Zeus is back and he is standing very close to her. The glasses are full and then they are empty. Jesse is looking at his collar, at his shoulder, at his neck, his ears. Now Zeus's hands are around her waist. She isn't holding her arms the way she practised with Artemis. She can feel his breath on her cheek, hot and damp. She closes her eyes. She can feel the bulge of his erection pressing against her. She wills herself not to feel anything down there. She has had erections before. It was horrifying. It was electrifying. She mentally cut it off, castrated herself. It cannot happen. She should go to the downstairs toilet and adjust herself but she cannot move. She is rooted to the spot, swaying with Zeus. Her head is swimming. She is underwater. She is in the sky. She is flying. She is floating.

9

Jesse's head hurts. She was passed out in Justin's downstairs toilet when Ana arrived last night. She remembers how small and cramped it was, with postcards on the walls and a tiny hanging mirror with a blue mosaic border that had been smashed, the cloying scent of pine filling her nostrils. She remembers banging her head on the hand basin in the corner as she sat on the toilet. Now Randy and her are both grounded. Ana is particularly angry with Randy, who was supposed to be doing the big brother thing and looking after Jesse.

"I still feel sick," whispers Jesse on the phone to Artemis the next morning, remembering that she puked and missed the toilet, that her mother had cleaned her up when they got home.

Jesse is still in bed in her pyjamas.

"It looked like you were really into Zeus last night," says Artemis. "Either that or you were just pretty hungry, the way you were eating his face off!"

Jesse tries to remember kissing Zeus. What it felt like, what he tasted like. But she can't remember anything apart from the vomit.

"How were things for you and Randy?" asks Jesse, propping herself up on one elbow and pulling the duvet up to her chin, even though it is summer.

"Eww! Are you asking me how far I went with your brother?!" screeches Artemis's voice down the phone.

"No! I just wondered whether you two were okay."

"Yeah, we're cool. So when are you gonna be allowed out? Ork's been asking about you."

Jesse manages to get out a few days later after Ana relents and decides that three days moping about the maisonette is enough for anyone.

"I suppose you had just finished your exams," said Ana on the third day. "You needed to let off a bit of steam."

"Yeah, Mum, it's what we do, so why were you such a bore about it?" snapped Randy, going stir crazy after three days of being cooped up like a chicken in a pen.

"Please don't use that tone with me, Randy," says Ana, raising her eyebrows, reminding herself that back chat is perfectly normal behaviour too.

Jesse feels nervous about seeing Ork again. She is worried about getting things wrong and forces herself not to think of him as a boy. 'Phe', she reminds herself, not 'he' or 'she'. She repeats the mantra as she walks down to the club with Artemis. Both girls are wearing jeans, tee-shirt and trainers. This time they go straight in together, no hanging about on fire exits. Jesse feels the soles of her trainers stick to the dirty floor as they go in. People mill about holding cans of drink, slopping fizz onto the floor. Jesse sees Max before she sees Ork. Today Max is dressed all in white, like a ghost with fire flowing from its head. Phers bright red hair is tangled on one side, the roots growing through in mousy brown, where the shaven side has started to grow back in short, downy tufts, like a duckling. Just when she thinks there is no sign of pink about Max today, Max bends over the pool table to take a shot and Jesse spots cerise ankle socks poking out of white plimsolls.

Her opponent, a fierce looking person with small, black eyes and pale skin, stares daggers at Jesse and Artemis, as they enter.

"Oh look, your little Halfie friends are here!" phe sneers.

Max looks over and a warm smile spreads over her face.

"Hi girls," beams Max, still holding the cue.

"Girls!" teases the black eyed opponent, putting on a high pitched voice.

Jesse hangs back, while Artemis rushes forwards to hug Max. It's then that Jesse notices some of Max's other tattoos: the number one on phers right forearm and a yin and yang symbol on phers left ankle, sitting just above the cerise sock.

"I hear you got up to a bit of party mischief the other day," says Max when it is Jesse's turn to greet pherm.

Jesse feels her face flush. She can't believe that Artemis has been blabbing again. She wonders whether Ork knows about her and Zeus and then wonders why she should even care.

"Why does phe call us Halfie?" asks Jesse once they are out of earshot.

"Oh, ignore the po-faced twat. Hunter isn't the most accommodating of people. Phe's harmless when you get to know pherm but phe likes to give it the big I Am. Hunter was christened Mary and raised as a girl until phe was five. Phe's got a bit of a chip on phers shoulder."

"So phe's had Assignment?" asks Jesse, confused, looking around to make sure Hunter isn't back within hearing range. People swarm past them. There seem to be so many here tonight.

"Not exactly. It was a botched operation, so phe's still got a small dick, or rather an enlarged clitoris as the medics call it. Phe hates men. Phe hates women. Calls you lot Halves. Well, not that you are. Yet."

Jesse stares open mouthed as Max talks so casually about enlarged clitorises. Is that what mine is, she wonders.

"Phe seems to forget the whole rationale behind We Are One," continues Max, unwrapping a Juicy Fruit and popping it into phers mouth. "Personally, I think we should be open to everybody but not everyone here sees it that way."

"We are one?" repeats Jesse, feeling she is missing vital information.

"The name of our group," says Max, shaking phers head. "Hasn't Artemis or Ork told you anything about us yet?"

"Not much," replies Jesse, giving Artemis a dirty look.

"You really need to talk!" she laughs.

"Why don't *you* tell me stuff then," asks Jesse, cutting Artemis out of her line of vision and fronting Max.

"Well, I'll tell you one thing as you don't seem to have the foggiest about anything. Ork was at the commune with us too. Do you remember?" Max stands back and assesses Jesse's reaction. "Oh, speak of the devil! Phe can tell you all about it phermself."

Jesse swivels round and sees Ork.

"Hi," says Ork, looking straight at Jesse and making her feel funny again.

She thinks back. Max and the pink bracelet yes, but Ork? She struggles to picture pherm there. Then she sees pherm. A small, quiet, dark haired child sitting in the corner. She never heard pherm speak.

"Can we talk?" asks Jesse.

Ork grins as though phe has been waiting for her to ask that very question. Phe leads her over to the worn sofas at the end of the hall. They sit down together.

"You were at the commune," says Jesse, sounding accusatory. "You never said."

"You never asked!"

Ork is still grinning. Jesse feels as though phe is playing with her, like a cat with a mouse.

"So, you and Max have been friends since you were kids?"

"Oh, we're not friends."

"Oh. So you don't like each other then. I thought you seemed quite close. The way Max talks about you…"

More smiles as Ork waits for her to catch on.

"Oh, you're together…" Jesse feels herself shrink as she realises they must be a couple.

"Not like that!" laughs Ork. "We're twins. Non-identical twins."

"Oh," Jesse smiles with pherm and wonders why she feels so happy about the revelation.

Ork fills her in on phers past. How Ork and Max are siblings. How they left the commune because their mum thought the rules were too restrictive.

"She got in a lot of trouble for letting Max wear pink. Pink contraband! I understand where they were coming from. They didn't want to push gender stereotypes down the throats of little kids by dressing them in pink and blue and giving them only dolls and cars to play with. But…" says Ork, playing with phers tweedy friendship bracelet.

Jesse looks at Ork's full lips as phe speaks and the way phers blue eyes change from sky to sea from sapphire to steel. She looks away and up at the black and white posters adorning the walls. Like stills from films but not the kind of films she has ever seen. There are no women in frilly skirts on the arms of men in suits. These are long, lean bodies in tight clothes and flowing clothes, sharp angles and soft lines all at once. Androgynous images.

"Mum wanted us to be able to show interest in things and follow our individuality without fear of reprimand. So what if Max likes pink? It doesn't make her a girl. The Natural Baby Movement is very limiting."

Phers words feel like a slap in the face. Jesse isn't used to anyone saying things like this about her mother's work. She understands that some gender assigned people can find the work of NBM threatening but Ork is not gender assigned. Surely Ana's work is pioneering. Controversial yes, but limiting? Surely it's the opposite of that?

"You know, you're not allowed to let the little kids say or do or wear anything that could be considered remotely gender stereotypical but then all of a sudden when they hit puberty, they jolly well better have decided which way they are going!" Ork stares at her defiantly. "Anyway, a group had already splintered off and set up another home. One of the teenagers had told phers parents phe didn't want to have Assignment, didn't want to choose to be girl or boy and why should phe?"

"I guess if someone doesn't want to choose…" Jesse trails off, fingering a worn patch on the sofa.

"Mum founded We Are One, with a group of ambi-gender people who do not identify themselves as exclusively female or male and believe that gender identity is irrelevant. We're a campaigning group who oppose the Natural Baby Movement, as well as the government."

"Oh," says Jesse, heat rising in her face. "And what exactly does this… your group, do to oppose my mother's work?"

"They campaign against Assignment and are fighting for a society where humans are left as intersex people and valued as individuals."

Jesse's head spins. Even though she doesn't like everything Ork is saying, she likes being spoken to as an intelligent, questioning, independent minded being.

"Our mother died of cancer five years ago," says Ork, looking down.

"I'm sorry," says Jesse, a picture of Max and Ork's mother popping into her head, a small, quiet woman, with red hair and a bright smile.

"It was a horrible time, the pain of watching someone you love die like that." For a moment, Ork looks far away, as though phe is remembering phers mother too. "It's important that we carry on her work. It's what she would have wanted."

"Yes, yes," says Jesse, nodding but not fully comprehending. "And do you… are you in contact with your father?"

"We never knew who our father was. To her dying day, Mum refused to tell us and as we never had our births registered, his name was never recorded anywhere. This is my family now." Phe gestures to the people around the room. "Several of us share a place. I live among friends. How about you? Is your dad around?"

"We're not in touch any more," says Jesse sadly, trying to conjure up an image of her father.

Ana doesn't keep photo albums. Apart from a small collection of framed photos adorning the walls of the maisonette, there is no record of their childhood. A hazard of moving so often; they've learned to travel light, to give things away, re-use, recycle. Never to hoard. It is so long since she saw him. She was only a toddler then. The image is blurry, without focus, more of a sensation than a picture. Arms round her shoulders. They are sitting on a bench somewhere, her face snuggled into his woolly jumper.

"But you knew him, right? You could probably track him down if you wanted to."

The idea startles Jesse. It's her and Randy and her mother now.

"You can stand up to your mother, you know," says Ork, taking Jesse aback yet again. "We'll support you."

"Oh, still chatting to the little, lost Halfie girl," shouts Hunter, suddenly appearing on the arm of the sofa. "Phe doesn't like Halves any more than me, you know. Phe's only talking to you because you haven't been mutilated yet. Thinks phe can save you."

10

Zeus is on the cracked doorstep a few days later. Standing there in broad daylight, beside the privet hedge, with his boyish grin and chunky arms, he looks younger, childlike, like an action figure or a cartoon character.

"Hi," he says, putting his hand to his face to shield his eyes from the sun.

"Hi," says Jesse, staring at him. Images from the party flash into her mind. Zeus's hands sliding round her waist. His mouth pressing onto hers. That's it, she remembers. Sensations flood through her: heat, electricity, dizziness. "Are you here for Randy? He's out right now. I can tell him he called by."

"No actually, I was here to see you," says Zeus, shuffling his white trainers backwards and forwards. "I hope you don't mind me coming by. I haven't heard from you since the party. I just wanted to check you were okay and everything. Randy said your mum went a bit mad."

A smile opens Jesse's face. "Yeah, we were both grounded. Thanks for the messages by the way."

A fly buzzes between them, making Jesse step backwards an inch. She laughs, looking down at her feet in her old, orange flip flops that she wears around the maisonette to stop bits of debris sticking to her bare feet. They stand there awkwardly, Zeus looking at Jesse looking at her feet.

"I had a good time at the party," he says, breaking the silence. "With you."

"Me too," says Jesse. "Hey, would you like to come in? I'm so rude!"

"Cool."

Zeus wipes his trainers on the frayed welcome mat and follows Jesse into the maisonette.

"There's nobody in. Mum's at work," she says, suddenly embarrassed. "Would you like a drink?"

"No, I'm cool, thanks."

He slouches and rests a hand on the battered sideboard. There is no space to move, the room is packed full of old furniture, everything squashed close together in the tiny room, making Zeus look like a giant again. Jesse stands beside the bean bag and sofa. She has never been completely alone with a boy before. She looks up at Zeus through her fringe and feels her cheeks burn. He has his hands in his jean pockets and he is still shuffling his feet, biting his bottom lip while smiling at her. His lips are chapped, his nose slightly sunburnt. The sun has lightened his closely cropped hair in places.

"Sit down!" she gushes, perching on the sofa, her heart pounding as he sits next to her.

The sunlight streams through the windows, illuminating the wooden ornaments on the side board. Ana has done the best she can to make the place look homely on a budget.

"So, what is it your mum does again?" asks Zeus, looking around the room. "Randy said she was like a social worker or something."

Jesse feels his eyes move over the worn patches in the sofa. Then his eyes move from the furniture to her face, catching her in his gaze. He picks up her hand and slowly interlocks their fingers. Jesse feels as though she is being electrified, every nerve ending in her body responds. She stares at their hands, entwined together.

Y-yeah, yeah, s-sort of," she stutters, as Zeus slowly starts stroking her fingers. "S-she works for a homeless charity."

She knows the drill. They are not allowed to tell anyone that Ana is involved with the NBM at Natural Souls. The homeless charity isn't a complete lie. Many of the pregnant women who come through its doors have to leave their homes to hide their babies from the world.

"Uh ha," says Zeus, staring at her mouth and leaning towards her.

Her heart rate quickens. She wills Randy to come home.

"And what about your parents?" asks Jesse, trying to keep the conversation going, panic rising in her chest.

"They're teachers, aren't they?" says Zeus, not taking his eyes of her mouth, his fingers now rhythmically stroking hers. Then, one hand frees itself and rests on her thigh and starts stroking through the cotton of her skirt.

"Oh yeah, of course!" she says, her voice rising, as she pulls away and stands up. "I should get you a drink. What will you have? Juice? Coke?"

"I really like you, Jesse," replies Zeus, standing and silently pulling her towards him, kissing her full on the mouth, his tongue parting her lips and exploring her mouth.

Jesse stands there frozen, feeling drawn into him and at the same time wanting to escape. His hands move over her body as he pulls her tighter into him. Then the bang of the front door and they quickly pull apart as Randy strides into the room.

"Hey, bro!" he shouts, slapping Zeus on the back. "I hope you aren't taking advantage of my l'il sis."

For a moment, Jesse wonders if she can trust Randy. He told Artemis that she hadn't been assigned. Who's to say he hadn't told Zeus? But then he wouldn't be hanging around, would he? Boys like Zeus don't date freaks like her.

Artemis and Jesse are in the mall. They wander around window shopping and people watching. Agitated mothers with screaming tots push buggies laden with bulging bags. Men in suits carrying briefcases march purposefully through the mall, expertly eating a sandwich lunch while conducting virtual business meetings. A very tall, broad shouldered girl walks out of a clothing store, clutching her newly acquired purchases in plastic bags. A feminine looking boy, petite in stature, with a soft face is browsing magazines in another shop window. For the first time, Jesse realises that this fantasy she has of perfect looking men and women is just that, a fantasy. Yes, most people have Gender Assignment at birth to fix their genital organs but the hormones and chromosomes aren't so easy to fix, not that that stops modern medicine from trying. Girls that look like boys and boys that look like girls are commonplace. Standing among the crowds, she feels that she fits in. Once she has her Assignment, she'll be no different from any of them.

They head to Superdrug to buy makeup, then loiter round the stands, trying tester lipsticks on the back of their hands.

"What about this one?" says Artemis, flashing a pillar box red streak on her wrist at Jesse.

"Hmm, maybe too bright. How about this?"

The operation is always at the back of Jesse's mind now, as it looms closer and closer, like Christmas. Jesse is looking forward to staying with Maya; they have always shared a special bond. She tries to focus on the afterwards. When she will be a proper woman. They will be staying by the coast. Maya moves about renting little places by the sea, says the sea air is the best thing for recuperating souls and bodies.

"Hey!" It is Deb, coming down the aisle towards them, blonde hair flouncing, her normally undefined waist clinched in with a wide silver belt over a black shirt.

"That's definitely your colour. Let's have a look."

She grabs Artemis's hand and pulls it towards her, turning it this way and that way, the lines of make-up shimmering under the store's spotlight. Artemis's mouth parts as she stares at Deb holding her hand. Her heavily mascaraed lashes start blinking faster than usual. Jesse watches as Artemis, who is usually so confident and vocal, turns quiet.

11

They have to get three buses to the old school, way out on the edge of town. The windows are smashed and boarded up, weeds thrive in the deserted playground, the building unused for decades, since the new school system was introduced, with boys and girls educated separately, in new buildings designed specifically to meet their needs. Girls' schools are fully equipped to deliver the Female Life Skills syllabus with state of the art facilities for domestic science, virtual baby dolls to assist girls in learning how to care for newborns. Boys' schools are renowned for their sporting amenities, and technical departments to assist in developing much needed vocational skills for young men in the making, who will be expected to support their families. Male Life Skills lessons stress the importance of responsibility, Female Life Skills the importance of nurturing and supporting.

When they finally arrive at the school hall, Jesse is tired and thirsty. Even Artemis looks drained, her usually bright eyes dull. They sit on plastic chairs at the back of the hall, barely speaking to one another. Jesse rummages around in her bag for a bottle of water. Then Ork is behind the mike, saying, "Testing, testing." Tonight, phe is wearing what passes as a suit, black jeans and a linen jacket, draped with phers characteristic multicoloured scarf. Phe looks even paler than usual and phers black eyeliner is even thicker. Max is fiddling with audio equipment and helping with the sound check. Phe wears a paisley jumpsuit, which surprises Jesse as it looks so feminine. She looks down at her baggy jeans and wishes she was wearing a dress, regretting changing her appearance to fit in. The place is seething and not just with the young people at the We Are One youth club. The room is filled with the sound of excited chattering, people coughing, children squealing and running up and down the aisle. Next to her sits an old person with wiry, grey hair and a beard. Phe clearly has boobs, which are not at all concealed in phers tight blue tee-shirt. She cannot stop looking and thinking, is this what Ork will become? Is this what she will become if she doesn't have the secret op that has been all planned out with Maya and the rest of the crew, the op that is oh so nearly upon her? Her stomach churns. Jesse steals a glance at Artemis, who is sitting on her hands. She desperately wants to get up and walk out but Ork is about to address the crowds that have gathered. Phers eyes scan the room but don't seem to register Jesse, who is sitting at the back. Jesse is glad that phe hasn't seen her. Maybe she can just sneak away without anyone noticing.

"Thank you all for coming to this special meeting of We Are One. It's so wonderful to see so many of our members, old and young, turned out today."

The person sitting next to Jesse jumps up and punches the air. "Here, here!"

"Thank you, Rowan." Ork's eyes find Jesse, next to the animated Rowan.

She slumps down in her chair and wishes she was invisible.

"In a hundred years' time, maybe even fifty, people will look back on this era in shock and disgust that Genital Mutilation, horrific abuse of innocent babies, was sanctioned by the government. By the time the grandchildren of today's youth are born, everyone will be free to live as a Whole person not a Half."

Jesse winces at the word, half. She recalls Hunter's twisted face as she mocked her, calling her a little, lost Halfie girl. Ork's hands are in phers pockets. Phe looks like a rock singer as phers full lips practically touch the mike.

"So what if intersex isn't what God or nature intended? There are a lot of things about modern society that aren't as God..." Phe looks around the room, "if you even believe there is a god that is – or nature intended. There's nothing natural about fitting pacemakers in hearts or talking to someone thousands of miles away through modern technology, is there? But nobody seems bothered about that. All species evolve and this is how the human species has evolved. We don't look like apes and we don't act like Neanderthals. We don't want to go back to a binary gender system any more than we want to revert to being cavemen. We are the Third Gender. Intersex is progress. Embrace it!"

"Here, here!" Rowan is off again.

"Hello darling. Have you had a good day?" Ana asks Jesse, looking up from reading her paper at the kitchen table.

Jesse loiters in the kitchen doorway, her bag hanging off her shoulder. Inside it contains the campaign literature that Ork handed out at the end of the meeting, with plans for protest action. Her back aches from sitting for so long on the uncomfortable plastic chair.

"Have you heard of a group called We Are One?" Jesse asks her mother quietly, answering her question with another question.

The colour drains out of Ana's face, her warm smile disappearing. "What do you know about those people?" she asks in a strained voice, hands forming fists over the crossword.

"A bit," replies Jesse, shrugging. "Artemis knows people there."

"Artemis!" exclaims Ana, her mouth forming an 'o' shape and refusing to close.

"Yeah but she didn't make me go there or anything. I wanted to know about…"

"You've been there! To that group!" Ana stands up and knocks her paper to the floor, the pages rustling through the air and hitting the lino with a gentle thud. "You must stay away from them, Jesse. They are not going to help you."

"Why? Why must I stay away from them?" Jesse feels agitated like she did in the hall earlier. She wanted to run away then and she wants to run away now.

"These people act against God," says Ana sternly, her face frowning as she picks up the paper and rearranges it on the table. "Everyone has an innate gender, Jesse. A true gender. It is just a case of discovering it. You know that. Everyone has their path."

"What if their true path is intersex?" challenges Jesse, her hands on her hips, her face set. "What if God made them that way? What if I don't even believe in God?"

Ana stares at her daughter, blinking wordlessly. Jesse doesn't move from the doorway.

"Ork says the Natural Baby Movement is very limiting." Jesse plays with her belt, awaiting her mother's response.

Ana laughs, a bitter laugh.

"What's so funny?" How dare her mother laugh at her.

"I don't want you to see those people."

"Tell me why." Jesse rubs the goosebumps on her arms, pulling her hoodie tightly around her.

"I will not discuss their actions, Jesse. I want you to trust me on this. I don't want you to see those people again."

"I'm nearly sixteen. You can't stop me." Eyes ablaze.

"How do you think these people will cope in society, living underground forever?" prompts Ana, sighing. "You know how hard it has been for you so far and now you are about to be set free! To become yourself! Imagine never finding that and living in the underworld forever. Our work is the opposite of limiting. We set people free! We expand lives. What roles do you think these people can play in society?"

"God, you sound like Mrs Pritchard," spits Jesse, her hands flying in front of her, making animated gestures. "All my life, all my life I thought you were pioneering, fighting injustice to help people but you're just like everyone else."

Ana's voice softens and she moves towards her daughter. "Are you worried about your Assignment? Is that it? Are you getting cold feet now it's been arranged? I do understand, you know…"

"You understand NOTHING!" shouts Jesse, bolting upstairs to her bedroom and locking the door, flinging herself on the bed and screaming and crying until there is nothing left to drain out of her, unsure why she is so upset, angry and afraid. And for the first time in a long time, Jesse wishes she could speak to her father and find out what he thinks about all this.

12

Since being elected as the leader of the youth group, Ork has delivered many speeches at We Are One but this time it's different. Phe has been asked to address the whole group tonight, not just the youth group. As phe walks out to face the crowd, phe is confronted by a sea of faces, kids, teens and adults, many familiar, some not so. Hunter is pacing the hall, hands in pockets, eyes darting up and down the rows of people assembled to hear Ork and the others, stopping to crouch down next to a seat and talk to someone, before rising and looking around for someone else to target. New recruit Jordan stands by the door, welcoming people to the hall with a smile but Ork can see phe has one eye out for trouble, shoulders tense under the leather jacket phe wears. In the front row, seasoned member Levi sits proudly, all bouncy curls and twinkly eyes, winking at Ork and tapping phers feet on the floor. The older members sit nearer the back. Look there's Drew and Kiran arguing again. Brogan, middle-aged and overweight, waves from below the blacked out window. Everyone is waiting. But it isn't just the older members that are making Ork nervous tonight.

Phe steps up to the mike. "Testing, testing."

Max puts a hand on phers arm, which phe acknowledges with a nod, communicating, I'm all right. Phe clears phers throat, listens to the noise in the hall simmer down as the crowd anticipates phers address. Phers hands shake. Phers mouth is dry.

"Thank you all for coming to this special meeting of We Are One. It's so wonderful to see so many of our members, old and young, turned out today."

Someone shouts, "Here, here!"

Ork's eyes continue to scan the room, recognising

65

more and more people all the time, as phe continues to talk, the words coming effortlessly from deep within, nerves fading away as passion takes over.

"Here, here!" Rowan is jumping in the air, beard bouncing.

Then Ork sees her. Sitting next to Rowan, arms curled round herself, eyebrows burrowed. When she sees pherm looking at her, she shrinks in her seat. Phe winces, noting her checking out the exit, but carries on talking, the practised words tumbling out of phers mouth, bypassing phers mind, which is full of her. Phe thinks of her at the commune, when she wasn't a her, not that she even is yet, not really, but it is how she has chosen to present herself to the world – as a girl. Why is she afraid of being phermself? All of phermself? He sees pherm running about in the garden with Max, playing ball, playing tag, while phe watched from the sidelines always the spectator, until their mother set up We Are One and phe found phers purpose in life. When Jesse walked into the youth group with Artemis that day not so long ago, Ork felt a connection between them. Phe wasn't imagining it, was phe?

"Good job," says Drew, during the refreshment break, slapping Ork on the back.

"Not that you were listening to most of it," says Kiran. "Too busy having a go at me."

Max pours glasses of cordial from a plastic jug. Blackcurrant, orange, lemon. Jordan stays by the door, peering outside. A small crowd gathers around Ork but phers eyes remain on Jesse, willing her not to leave. Phe sees her rise from her seat, Artemis saying something to her then waving.

"Thanks, thanks," phe mutters. "Sorry, I need to talk to someone."

Phe strides purposefully over to where Artemis and Jesse now stand, Jesse's body pointing towards the door.

"Hi," phe says. "I'm glad you both came."

"That was quite a speech you gave." Artemis, trying to be positive.

Ork watches Jesse. She doesn't make eye contact.

"What did you think, Jesse?"

"Yeah, it was interesting," she replies, looking at the floor.

"Are you sticking around for the second half? We have some really good speakers coming up."

The second half of the meeting passes in a blur. Hunter steps up to the mike, hands still deep in pockets.

"My name is Hunter but I was christened Mary," phe stutters, looks down.

Phe doesn't look up until phe is finished telling pher story. Ork wipes tears from the corner of phers eyes. Hunter, so usually full of anger and hatred, stripped bare, revealing phers vulnerability. Ork is so proud of pherm. Max, Drew, Brogan. Story after story. All different. All the same. The pretence. The secrecy. The shame. The pain and suffering inflicted by having to live in society as something other than they are. As Ork listens to the familiar stories from the side of the stage, phe studies Jesse, looking for her reactions, something to indicate that this is affecting her, that these voices, these stories are changing her mind about having Assignment. She stays slumped down, peering up through her fringe from time to time to glance at the speakers, never looking at pherm. Every time she shuffles in her seat or moves her head, phe wonders what it means, what she's thinking. Now Jordan's turn, standing there, not removing phers armour despite the heat, the heavy leather jacket that covers and protects.

"My name is Jordan. Like Hunter, I had Assignment at birth too but mine wasn't botched."

The room falls silent. You could hear a pin drop. Not everyone at We Are One is comfortable with gender assigned people. But Ork is most interested in Jesse's reaction.

"I was assigned as a girl."

Ork sees Jesse sit up straighter now, her eyes trained on Jordan. Phe looks at Jordan as though seeing pherm for the first time. Would phe look like a girl to a Half? Phers chin length, dark hair curls softly around phers face, phers biker leathers hide phers body. When phe speaks, phers voice is soft and quiet, but throaty. Ork isn't sure how phe would be perceived now, although phe knows from Jordan first-hand how phe has been perceived in the past.

"I was okay about it at first," says Jordan, shoulders raised, hand clutching the microphone as though it is a weapon. "My parents were quite liberal. They never trussed me up in frilly dresses or anything like that anyway. When I was about twelve, I started fancying people assigned as boys. I had a boyfriend called Keith who kissed me behind the bike shed. All the usual stuff."

There is a chuckle from the audience and then coughing, as though trying to disguise their laugh for fear of being inappropriate. Ork watches as Jesse leans into Artemis's hair and whispers something in her ear, desperate to know what is said.

"But as my body developed, I started feeling that everything was wrong. My breasts felt alien to me. I felt as though I didn't belong in my changing body. It was as though I was trapped in someone else's body. It's so hard to explain but I just wanted to climb out of my skin. It was a feeling I'd never had before. I knew then that it would kill me to go on living as a woman."

Jesse and Artemis are deep in whispered conversation now, no longer looking at Jordan. There is silence and Ork realises that Jordan is looking nervously over at pherm. Phe nods, *go on*.

"So I moved home and started over, living as a teenage boy, a young man, but with female genitals, which I kept a secret. It was a relief to discover that I didn't have to be a woman despite having been assigned as one. I, I…" Phe hesitates and looks round the room. "For a long time, I have been considering going through a sex change transition to be reassigned male."

There is a gasp. Ork sees some of the members shake their heads in disapproval. Jesse is watching Jordan intently.

"I'm new to We Are One but now I am learning about amigendered people and I am not sure any more whether I need to have a sex change. I'm just not sure how important my body actually is in all this. I hope I can move to a place of self-acceptance here. Maybe, even a place where I can have a loving relationship with an ambigendered person, someone who really understands how I feel, even though I am a Half."

Hunter moves forward to speak, the hard edge in phers eyes returned. Ork steps in.

"Thank you so much for sharing that, Jordan. And thank you to all our speakers and to everyone assembled here tonight. I would like to finish the speeches with some closing remarks. If the government outlaws Gender Assignment, then we wouldn't need to live underground. We wouldn't be treated as freaks, have to live away from our families for fear of them being prosecuted for our existence, for not having their babies assigned. We don't want to feel like freaks. We don't want to be a minority group. Everyone should be left intersex. We are the Third

Gender. We are all the same. We Are One!"

"Here, here!" Rowan is jumping up again.

Jesse is standing up and trying to make her way past Rowan.

"Hey, are you coming down to the club next week? We're going to hold the youth group meeting to discuss the next steps."

Phe wants to ask what she thought of Jordan's speech but it's not the right time for a discussion like that, not tonight in front of all these people. They can talk next week at the club. They'll find a quiet corner, a quiet moment and talk. Really talk. Phe'll make pherm understand.

"Sorry, I can't," says Jesse. "I'm going away for the summer."

Ork stares at her, panic rising in phers chest.

"What for?" phe asks, although phe already knows the answer.

"It's summer!" says Jesse, waving her hands dismissively. "Can't a girl go away on holiday?"

The word 'girl' flutters through the air and lands between them pushing them apart.

"Where are you off to? Anywhere nice?" Ork's body feels heavy. She's going to do it. It's too late.

"Oh, just off to stay with family. Anyway, I'd better go," says Jesse, her lips folding into a smile that doesn't meet her eyes.

"Jesse!" Ork calls after her as she turns on the heels of her plimsolls, walking towards Artemis who is already at the door.

"What?"

The unspoken words beat in phers chest, bursting to come out.

"Don't do it, don't let them mutilate you!"

"Stay whole, not half!"

"Don't do this to yourself! Don't do this to me!"

But all phe says is, "Have fun then."

"I'll try," replies Jesse, holding phers gaze for a few moments.

"Don't do anything I wouldn't do." She just about hears as she make her way outside with Artemis.

13

"Take care of her," says Ana standing on the doorstep in her fluffy, yellow dressing down, wiping tears from the corners of her eyes as she hugs Jesse.

"Of course," says Maya, winking to Ana. "You know I will."

"Mum!" says Jesse. "You're squeezing me to death!"

The air is crisp and breezy this morning, the mini heat wave they have been experiencing over for now. Jesse thinks a storm might be brewing and hopes Maya can drive through it safely. She doesn't want anything delaying their journey today. Ana kisses Jesse, handing her neatly packed holdall, nerves written all over her face.

"I'll be fine, Mum."

After their argument the other day, Jesse worried that things would be forever changed between them. But the next morning, they both carried on as though nothing had happened, no angry words had been spat out. Jesse sat at the dining table, eating marmalade on toast and asking Ana where she would be staying afterwards.

"Maya's sorted somewhere nice and private for you," replied Ana, patting Jesse on the head and fluffing up her hair. "She'll look after you."

It was almost normal… except Jesse could sense her mother's eyes burning into her at every turn, unspoken question marks hanging in the air.

"Jesse," she began, leaning against the sink, turning a spoon over in her hand.

Jesse looked up at her mother. Her worry lines were getting deeper, she thought.

"You won't…"

It was the question that never got asked, as Randy tore

into the room, asking whether anyone had seen the remote control.

Jesse waves out of the back window as Maya's battered, white Beetle drives slowly down the road, not taking her eyes off Ana's until they turn a corner and their connection is broken.

"How are you feeling?" asks Maya, peering over her wire rimmed glasses with a look of concern, scruffy hair flying out of the tortoise shell grip trying in vain to contain it.

"I don't really know," replies Jesse, staring out of the window as the town fades behind them, grey concrete making way to trees and fields.

"It's okay to be scared," says Maya gently, flicking the car stereo on.

Rock music blares out, filling the space, filling Jesse's head with a rhythmic banging punctuated by the occasional scream. She is grateful not to have to talk, to be alone with her thoughts. Her mother would be playing something supposedly calming now. Classical or soft jazz to chill her out. Jesse can't quite bring herself to tell her mother that it always has the opposite effect on her, the quiet order making her panic. The noise and chaos in Maya's car relaxes her, makes her own mind feel at peace. She closes her eyes and feels herself drift, falling, falling…

There is Zeus, hands all over her, leaning into her, kissing her neck, murmuring sweet nothings in her ear, making her feel alive and dead at the same time. Artemis at the mall, staring at Debra, proffering her hand, smudges of colour streaked all over it, a startled expression on her face. Ork. Bright eyes staring out from phers pale face, searing her. *Everyone will be free to live as a Whole person not a Half.* Phers multi-coloured scarf unravelling and falling away to reveal phers body beneath. Jesse runs her hands over phers smooth, muscular chest. Ork as a boy. Then the scarf whips up and around him, spinning him round and round like a ballerina before falling away once more to reveal small but perfectly formed breasts, ripe and soft. The scarf is over Jesse's face now, suffocating her, winding round her neck, strangling her. Her mother's face, eyes watching but doing nothing.

The building is hidden behind dense rows of sycamore trees, overladen with thick, bushy, green leaves. As the car draws into the dusty clearing, Jesse sees Jordan, in phers heavy, leather jacket, holding the mike. *For a long time, I have been considering going through a sex change transition to be reassigned male.* She wonders what Jordan will do, whether phe will be driven to a place like this, a hidden clinic masquerading as a warehouse in the middle of nowhere. Will a friend of Jordan's drive phers out into the country for miles in a battered, old car like this? Or will phe decide not to do it? Will We Are One convince Jordan otherwise? Jesse wonders if Jordan's mother knows that her daughter has been living as a boy, has been considering a sex change and is now at home with intersex people, ambigendered people. She wonders if they still talk, if they are okay, and suddenly she realises just how much her own mother's acceptance means to her. But is that the reason she is doing this?

Maya parks up and leads Jesse out of the car, holding her hand.

Are you having Tom Donald Browne? He's the best, you know. And very discreet. She imagines Jo, fluttering her diamante nails, walking ahead of her up the gravel path to the small door.

I wouldn't go to Browne. I've heard bad things about him. Ash, small and mousy, jumps out from behind a tree, grabbing her arm.

"I don't know if I can!" shrieks Jesse, boots digging into the path, body rigid with fear. "Maya, I don't know!"

Jesse feels like she is being submerged in water, lungs filling rapidly, drowning, her heart bursting out of her ribcage.

"Shh, come on, you'll be fine. Let's get inside now." Quiet, reassuring, still holding her hand.

Maya rummages around in her bag and pulls out a translucent key ring, dry, pressed flowers trapped between the sheets of plastic. They enter through a side door and Maya opens a second, smaller door to a hidden basement. This is no ordinary basement, more like a tunnel, where a narrow, winding pathway leads them further down into the underworld. The air is stuffy and thick, pressing in on her ears and filling her mouth like cotton wool. Jesse's pupils widen in the dark as she follows Maya, her breathing becoming shallow as she walks down endless flights of stairs until her thighs ache so much, she knows there is no way back up.

At the bottom, they are greeted by a small Asian woman wearing a crisp white overall and a serious looking smile. Her long, dark hair is tied back into an elegant bun and she wears cerise lipstick.

"Hello Jesse. I'm Dr Shah," she says, putting out a slim, crinkly hand, which Jesse tentatively shakes. Dr Shah opens the door to a small operating theatre, a startling white, bright light blinding Jesse, the smell of antiseptic flooding her nostrils. She blinks and refocuses to see a clean and tidy room, a small white bed in one corner, a thin, wiry man holding a clipboard beside it. "And this is my assistant, Mr Rhodes. He will draw your blood to check your health, and place electrodes on your chest to measure your heart function."

Mr Rhodes nods at Jesse. He does not look like an unkind man but still Jesse does not want him drawing her blood. Vampire.

"There will be a bowel prep to clean out your intestines," continues Dr Shah, after gesturing for Jesse and Maya to sit on the plastic chairs arranged in one corner, as a makeshift consulting room. Jesse looks around at the bare walls and wonders how long this place has been used for what it is about to be used for. Are they just here for today? Does the clinic move about, some kind of gender fixing roadshow? "This will help prevent problems during the surgery and also give you a couple days of rest so you don't have to strain to go to the bathroom afterwards. The area that will be operated on will need to be shaved."

Jesse sees Jordan, Ash and Jo in front of her, now in backless hospital gowns. They are all talking to her at once so she cannot understand what they are saying but she knows they are arguing. Her head hurts. She knows they are not real, just imaginings, the product of fear, but she wants to know what they are saying all the same. She sees Jo on the bed now, smiling, patting the mattress and beckoning Jesse to join her. Jesse stares as Mr Rhodes places one hand on the tall, wooden screens and starts to move them across, obscuring the view.

14

The shriek of the seagulls wakes her. Still groggy from sleep, Jesse opens her eyes and props herself up, looking around. She is lying fully clothed on the bottom bunk of a narrow bunk bed covered in a chintzy throw. The metal frame creaks as she moves and a pain sears through her. It's over, she thinks. I am a woman now. She recalls the blur of the clinic. Dr Shah smiling at her and telling her not to worry about a thing. She remembers coming out of the anaesthetic, hooked up to a machine that administers pain relief, falling in and out of dreams full of Zeus and Ork and Randy and George and Debra and Ana and Mrs Pritchard. She remembers Dr Shah showing her her new body, the redness of the incisions, held together with adhesive tape, the strangeness of her new shape down below.

And now she is here, in the middle of wherever on a chintz bunk bed. Her right hand creeps slowly down over her abdomen but stops just above her pubic bone.

"Jesse!" calls Maya's voice through the door. "Are you awake? Can I come in?"

Jesse rubs her eyes and looks around the room. It is tiny with a small, pine chest of drawers in the corner and nothing else.

"Yeah, come in," croaks Jesse.

The door opens and Maya steps in, wearing a faded peach velour tracksuit, her auburn hair tied up in a bun on the top of her head. There are two pink spots on either cheek.

"I thought I heard you moving about. How are you feeling, pet?"

"Okay," says Jesse, noticing a kitchenette running outside the doorway, a hob and a microwave and a small sink. Jesse realises she is in a caravan. Then remembers arriving last night. Sleeping stretched out in the back of Maya's car, feeling jolts of pain every time she drove over a bump in the road, being helped out of the car half asleep and numb with pain, no longer hooked up to the medication, stumbling into the caravan and into bed. "Where am I?"

"Down by the coast, my love. Home sweet home for a good few weeks while you recuperate." Maya hands her some pills and a glass of water. "Take these. I'll supplement the medication with some herbs later. Now do you want anything to eat? Scrambled egg do you?"

Maya brings Jesse's food on a tray and sits on the floor by the bed while she eats. Jesse looks out of the windows at the sand dunes, covered in tufts of long grass, and the pebbly beach stretching out to a wild, grey sea. Further along the coast, Jesse sees a row of pastel coloured beach huts – powder blue, soft pink, pale green, lemon yellow – miniature in the distance, with triangular roofs like little dolls' houses. She imagines people inside the huts, changing out of their wet swimwear, discarding salty, sodden Lycra on the floor and wrapping themselves in fluffy towels. Soon, she'll be able to get changed without worrying about her secret being discovered. She'll be carefree and girlish like all the others.

Maya looks over at Jesse taking in the sights.

"A room with a view, eh? We were lucky this time. Called in a favour. We're quite secluded here though, far enough away from the main thrust for you to get some peace and quiet to help you rest."

The days pass in a blur of eating, sleeping and reading. By the second week, Jesse is able to transfer to the living room area to recline on the pull out sofa and watch crap, daytime TV shows. Maya fusses around her, busying herself in the kitchen, making soups and brews that promote healing. Sometimes, Maya goes out leaving Jesse alone, feeling both liberated and afraid, walking slowly to the cramped bathroom, with its mouldy tiles and dripping shower, locking the door and inspecting the changes in her body, every day a little more healed. Every day closer to being free and whole. She has a flashback of Hunter calling her a lost Halfie girl, then the sound of Ork – *Everyone will be free to live as a Whole person not a Half* – and pushes it away.

Finally, Maya says she is ready to go for a walk. They go out early in the morning before the day has properly started, while the beach is deserted and still. The sea air hits Jesse's face and nostrils as she steps out of the caravan, the rush and roar of the sea calling to her. They walk barefoot over the pebbles, Jesse holding onto Maya's arm, laughing at the thrill of being outside. Once they have braved the sharpness of the stones, there is the treat of gravelly sand, softer on the foot and ever nearer the waves. Two sets of footprints trail along the beach in front of them all the way along the shore, large sturdy boot shaped prints next to paw marks. Jesse can just about make out the shape of the figures way in the distance, the man with his dog by his side.

As they make their way nearer to the water's edge, the sea spray hits their ankles. Jesse gasps as the cold foam creeps over her feet, feeling a sudden urge to wade out into the depths of the water and feel the sting of the sea salt against her new body, to be at one with nature. Instead, she grips Maya's hand and squeezes it tightly, smiling at the older woman. Maya's hair is loose and frizzy, blowing in the breeze, her white shirt billowing around her. Two women hand in hand paddling in the sea.

Jesse turns her face up to the early morning sun, closing her eyes. Then the shriek of the gulls as they descend, swooping past Jesse's face, startling her, their black beady eyes searching.

15

While Maya pops out alone a few days later, Jesse scours the caravan. They must be sharp enough to cut properly. There are no scissors to be found in the kitchen drawer. She picks up a bread knife, turning it over in her hand, running the serrated edge softly against the tips of her fingers and wondering if she can do it with that instead. But no, it is scissors she needs. She feels bad entering Maya's bedroom and going through her things. Her room is about the same size as Jesse's but houses just a single bed, not a bunk. Maya slept above Jesse for the first couple of nights, always there, always on hand, but then retreated, allowing them both some privacy. It is the first time Jesse has been in here. Maya's purple, towelling dressing gown falls off the hanger on the back of the door as Jesse enters, crumpling to the floor and preventing the door from fully opening. Jesse stands by the partially open door reconsidering her actions but the pull is too strong. Pushing the door open and picking up the robe, she takes in the mess. Maya's bag lies in the middle of the small room, unzipped, guts spilling out, screwed up clothes pouring down its sides. Another bag on top of the pine chest, a pink, flowery plastic bag, the kind that normally contains toiletries. Jesse moves over to the bag and picks it up. She finds blister packs of pills. She knows what they are. Hormones. In the absence of any discussion to the contrary, Jesse had always assumed that Maya was like Ana, born female. She wonders when Maya had Assignment. Was it at birth? It strikes her as strange that she has never spoken about it considering that she has chosen to dedicate her life to the cause. Is she still embarrassed about it? Ashamed? Then, what she is looking for, the scissors. She holds them in her hand, feeling powerful,

81

then carefully replaces things as they were, before leaving the room.

She is in the commune, standing on a chair looking out of a window at snow falling. Randy is beside her fidgeting, looking far away as though he would rather be running about in the snow not cooped up at the table. And now she sees Ork too, folding white paper into squares and passing it to her. Phe is cutting out shapes with child-friendly scissors as Jesse watches. She still can't handle scissors properly. When phe is finished, phe opens out the paper and Jesse stares at the most beautiful paper snowflake, her eyes glittering like the ice outside.

"Show me!" she says and phe does, taking her hand and showing her how to use the scissors properly.

She feels warm and happy. They spend the afternoon making paper snow while Randy and Max run outside with a ball. Then Ork's mother comes to the table with a tray of steaming mince pies, sweet and fruity. They are coming thick and fast now, the memories. Meeting Ork and Max again after all those years seems to have triggered something somehow, to have opened the floodgate to pictures, sounds, smells and tastes long forgotten.

She stands in front of the tiny bathroom mirror, staring at her reflection, noticing how much she has changed since those days of unisex haircuts and khaki shirts. *I don't need to pretend to be a girl any more.* She holds up a lock of shoulder length hair and snips, watching it fall to the floor. A sense of release runs through her. Grabbing together a fist of hair now, she chops. And chops. Adrenaline pumping, all the while watching her old self fall away in the mirror and her new self be born. When she is done, Jesse confronts the person staring back at her, tufts of hair framing her face, softening her jaw. Elfin. She takes the scissors to her room and pulls dresses and skirts from her holdall, cutting them into pieces and throwing them up in the air, watching them flutter around her, feeling as high as if she was showering under hundred pound notes. She chops the bottoms off her jeans and rolls them up. Nothing should stay as it was. Dismayed at her girlie attire, she can find nothing to put on top. She sees the black tee-shirt on the washing line, the one that Maya has been wearing in bed, freshly washed and dried in the sun. Hopping out of the caravan with her silk robe pulled round her shoulders, she snatches the tee-shirt from the line and runs back inside. Pulling it on, she feels better. This is the new Jesse.

"Hi," says Jesse as soon as Maya enters her sight.

She has been sitting on the caravan steps, basking in the late afternoon sun for the last hour.

Maya's mouth hangs open as she takes in Jesse's new look.

"I hope you don't mind me borrowing the tee-shirt. Nothing of mine seemed to fit."

"It's no problem," says Maya, worry lines forming across her forehead. "As long as you're okay?"

"I'm cool," says Jesse grinning. "I feel much better like this."

Maya's lines disappear, a slow smile spreading across her face, before becoming serious.

"You know, Jesse. If you ever need any help, I'm not just talking about now but ever in the future, you know you can always come to me, always. No matter if you fall out with your mum, Lord knows I fell out with mine, I'm always here for you. Things aren't always black and white. People are more important than causes, Jesse. Just remember if you ever need me."

Mothers and daughters, thinks Jesse, dismissing Maya's offer as something she'll never need.

There is peace in solitude but loneliness too. It was agreed that nobody but Maya would know about their whereabouts. Not Randy, not even her mother. Jesse was forbidden from telling anyone. "Whatever you do, don't go telling that Artemis girl anything," Ana had instructed sternly before confiscating her phone, to prevent temptation getting the better of her. Jesse lies on the top bunk of her bed and thinks about Ork, wonders what she will say to pherm when she sees pherm again. Wonders if she will be welcome at the group now she is a Halfie. Having so much time to think leaves her brain talking to itself, going round and round previous conversations and inventing future ones. On her last night at the caravan, Jesse cannot sleep. Tomorrow she will be going home, back to her mother and brother and all her friends. Back to Zeus. And Ork. Soon she will be going to sixth form college. Her mother will not like her new image, her teachers neither. They will say she is not presenting herself properly, she should take more care of her personal grooming. The Female Life Skills Syllabus bangs on about stupid stuff like that. Artemis will think it is cool. And Ork?

Jesse wakes and moves to the window, pulling back the thin curtain to look at the full moon. Her period will come soon. She stands by the window and looks out for a while, until tiredness overcomes her. Closing the curtain and moving back to the bed, she sees a bulge in the top bunk. Confused, she moves closer, knowing she was sleeping on the bottom bunk, knowing she had left the top bunk neatly made up before she went to bed. Perhaps Maya came in and threw a duvet on the top bunk in case she needed it. After all, it had felt cooler today, and she's complained in the morning of draughts giving her neck ache. Climbing up the wooden ladder, she reaches out, to smooth out the duvet, to get everything in order so she can go back to sleep, to prepare herself for her big day tomorrow. Her return.

Her hand hits warm flesh. A thigh. Jesse gasps. Maya must have decided to sleep in with her tonight. Maybe she thought she'd need company tonight. But it isn't Maya. As her eyes travel over the body in the bed, she sees something shocking. Herself. Lying on the top bunk is Jesse as a boy.

16

Randy stands in the hallway, watching his mother clean. She has been cleaning every day this week, dusting away debris, polishing every surface in the house until it gleams, smoothing over creases in the throws, darning curtains. It's maddening, this amount of cleaning. It's not normal. He can barely finish his cereal these days before she whisks the bowl away and wipes down the table. He feels he is being erased, wipe by wipe. Ana stands now, mop in hand, about to clean the bathroom lino.

"Mum, I need to go out," says Randy, wondering if she's even listening to him. He fidgets as he stands there, leg twitching, hands moving.

Ana turns to face him.

"Where? For how long? You know Jesse is coming home today. I want us to both be here to greet her. I'm making a special homecoming meal."

It's all about Jesse. Ana has barely spoken to him since Jesse left, just pined for her daughter-to-be. Every minute of every day, she's been preparing for Jesse's homecoming. Yesterday, she went out shopping and came back with a fancy carrier bag. She had beamed as she showed Randy the posh new dress it contained, slowly taking the red silk dress out of its wrapper and holding it up to the mirror. Sometimes, Randy wishes it was he who was chosen to be the girl.

"Just somewhere. Not long." Randy shrugs.

"Have you and Artemis been fighting again?"

He's sure he can detect pleasure in his mother's voice.

"I know it's difficult, darling, but maybe it just isn't to be," ventures Ana, leaning on the mop. "First love is always special but it rarely lasts. Maybe you and Artemis have run your course."

"I'm going out." He moves down the hall and the front door bangs behind him.

Halfway down the road, he sees Maya's car. He stands by the wall so Jesse cannot see him as she steps out of the car. He's not ready to see her yet. Ana runs down the path and flinches. He sees the frozen look on her face before he sees Jesse.

Ork is in the kitchen attempting to fix the drinks machine, or rather bashing it hard with phers fists in the hope that it will restart. The place could do with a finance injection, the facilities are definitely past their best before date, but there is no money for underground projects like this. It's not as though they can exactly apply to the government for a subsidy like other community projects. Corporate sponsorship is out of the question too. Instead, they have to rely on members' donations to keep going on their shoestring budget. The machine starts spluttering to life, hot water spurting out the front and burning Ork's fingers.

"Hi there," comes a voice from behind pherm.

Phe knows that voice anywhere. Phe turns round, sucking phers fingers, and looks at Jesse, barely recognisable from before. Phe blinks and takes in her appearance, the mismatched image phe holds of her in phers mind superimposing itself on this real version of Jesse. As phe looks at her cropped hair and bare face, denim shirt and three-quarter length black cargo pants, the hairs on phers arm stand to attention.

"There's no need to look so shocked," laughs Jesse, running her hand through her new hair.

"I, I…" Ork cannot take phers eyes off her.

The new Jesse looks totally at home at We Are One. Gone are the long hair and lipstick but it's not just that. Her whole demeanour has changed. Whereas before she walked about stiffly, eyes darting about the room, face taught, now she moves with grace and ease and a relaxed smile.

"You're speechless! I guess you like my new look then?"

Ork is confused. Phe was expecting her to come back looking even more like a girl, now that she has cut off the other half of herself. Unless…

"So…?" Ork stares at her and something shifts. The connection phe thought phe might have imagined resurges. There will be time for questions later. "Hey, mind my manners. Would you like a cup of tea or something now I've got this old thing working again?"

"Sure. I brought some hot chocolate powder with me. Mum won't miss it," says Jesse shrugging. "Want some?"

"How is your mother?" *Meaning: How has she react-ed to the new you? Who is the new you?*

"She's okay," says Jesse, setting about making the drinks, not giving anything away.

Why do you look like that? Did you change your mind and realise that you don't have to be half a person? Is this your way of telling me that you understand, that you are like me, that you like me, that We Are One?

They take their drinks over to one of the sofas in the corner. The club is quiet tonight. People are recovering from the frantic activity of the last few weeks. Organising the petitions and sending them to Parliament. Kiran and Drew have been designing the We Are One badge and sash in preparation for the next stage. To show they are serious. Jesse asks how things have been going with the group and Ork fills her in on their recent activity.

"Where's Artemis tonight?" asks Ork, glancing about. Jesse has never been here without Artemis before.

"She's not feeling too well but I wanted to see you so I

came by myself. I'm a big girl now!"

Girl. Girl. Girl.

"So you, you went through with it then?"

A shadow passes across Jesse's face. "Of course."

"Right, right. Well, I have to get on. I've got a lot to organise," phe says, standing up and knocking phers cup onto the floor.

Phe sees the hurt in Jesse's face, knows phe is being cold but cannot help it.

"Don't you want to know how it went?" asks Jesse in a quiet voice. "How I feel now?"

Ork looks at her for a long moment. "Not really, no."

17

"Not really, no."

So, there it is. Ork isn't interested in me anymore, thinks Jesse. I was kidding myself to think that we could still be friends afterwards.

"Oh, okay. I'll let you get on then."

Jesse stands slowly, staring into Ork's eyes. Then when she cannot bear it any longer, she looks down at the broken cup on the floor, the dregs of the hot chocolate forming a gooey puddle on the lino. Such a mess.

I should never have come here. I don't belong here. Not any more.

Ork's face haunts her during the long walk home, the way phers eyes contracted when phe realised she'd had the operation. She had felt so stupid when she realised that Ork thought she'd changed her mind and come back to declare that she was joining We Are One. It hadn't occurred to Jesse that phe might interpret her new image in that way. As she heads nearer to home and starts to see other people on the streets, Jesse feels people looking at her. She starts to have trouble breathing, her chest feels tight.

Am I still a freak?

The first time it happened, on the bunk beds, Jesse was freaked out. But she has become used to seeing the other half of herself now. At first, she thought he was a dream but now she is not so sure what he is. Another product of her over active imagination? A manifestation of some kind? A ghost? If half of you dies, is there half a soul left floating somewhere? Sometimes, she sees him getting out of the bed before her when she wakes up. He walks over to the bedroom door, legs strong and muscular, then he turns to look at her and disappears. Sometimes, she sees him last thing at night, leaning over her, telling her everything will be okay. She hasn't told anyone about it. They'd all think she was mad. She can't imagine telling her mother something like that. Or Randy or Artemis. And certainly not Zeus. He definitely wouldn't understand. He has only ever been what he is now. She wonders whether Hunter or Jordan would understand and whether she can go back to We Are One to see them. Now he is here again, in the bath, squeezed in next to her quite amiably, soaping his back while she shaves her legs, running her hands along her smooth skin. She watches him closely. Every day he looks a little different. Today, he has stubble. He reaches over and takes her razor, turning it over in his hands, then slowly shaving it off. His jaw looks a little squarer, his Adam's apple bigger, his chest broader. She is not afraid of him but she would like to talk to someone who also sees their other half. He passes her the razor back with a smile and she does her other leg.

"Jesse!" calls her mother, through the bathroom door, and he slips under the water and vanishes. "Zeus is on the phone, checking you're still on to be picked up at seven. Shall I tell him you'll call him back?"

She tells herself that things will be easy with Zeus. He won't ask difficult questions and make her feel wrong about herself. When she is with him, she will be like any other girl, walking arm in arm with her boyfriend. Like Debra and Derek. A normal couple. After the reaction from her mother and Ork, Jesse decides to make an effort for their re-union. She steps out of the bath and watches the water drain away, no sign of her other half now. Wrapping herself in a towel, she decides her hair needs softening before she goes out and rummages through the bathroom cupboard for the heated rollers that her mother often uses. Her make-up bag is full of the wrong stuff, all pastels. She wants dark, striking colours, something to make a statement. She pulls out some of the cosmetics she bought with Artemis that time they bumped into Debra. More like it. Smoky eyes and barely-there lips. She thinks something tight will be right for tonight, now she doesn't have to worry about concealing anything under her skirt. Tight black satin pants and a black lacy blouse. Taking out the rollers and fluffy her hair out, she faces herself in the mirror. It's not the old, sugary sweet Jesse. It's not the androgynous, plain Jesse either. This is sexy Jesse, someone she's never seen before.

"Darling!" says her mother as Jesse emerges from her bedroom in a cloud of perfume. "You look wonderful."

Jesse smiles. She remembers her mother's words from a few months before. *He's a proper teenage boy your brother... I'm so pleased for him that he has finally become himself.* And she hopes her mother feels the same about her. A proper teenage girl, that's what she finally feels like tonight.

When Jesse opens the door to Zeus, he looks startled.

"Hi," she says, running her hands down her thighs and wondering if the trousers are too tight.

"Wow," he says smiling, hands in his pockets. "You should go away more often."

"Absence makes the heart grow fonder?" she teases.

His eyes travel over her body. "Yeah. You look different. You look really great."

"Thank you. You're not so bad yourself." Jesse's heart beat speeds up in anticipation of later. She knows exactly what will happen tonight.

They go to see a film but Zeus watches only her. She can feel his eyes moving over her body, her cheeks burn under his gaze. Actors run about shooting people, bombs go off, people scream, but Jesse sees nothing. Zeus's hand slowly snakes it way over to her leg and slowly he traces a finger up her thigh. Her breathing changes.

"You look so sexy tonight," he whispers in her ear, gently nibbling her neck and turning her face to kiss him full on.

Popcorn spills onto the floor and for a moment, Jesse thinks of Ork and the hot chocolate but she pushes the thought away. They kiss for ages, hard, hungry kisses, teeth bashing. She never knew kissing could taste this good. When they pull apart, Zeus's eyes are glazed, his lips swollen.

"Do you want to go somewhere?" he murmurs.

They stare into each other's eyes, the question hanging in the air. People munch popcorn and slurp coke around them. Actors talk on the screen. A hunky policeman chats up a glamorous redhead. Jesse nods and Zeus leads her out of the auditorium by the hand. Everything is going exactly to plan. Her whole body pulsates as he pulls her along the street, looking at her, up and down. Every now and then they stop and he pushes her against the wall, leaning into her, murmuring, kissing her neck, tugging at her hair, making electricity. She doesn't speak but lets him think he is in control. A man walks past with a dog and they stop, standing there panting while they pass. Jesse laughs but Zeus looks serious.

"I know where we can go where we won't be disturbed. This way."

He leads her down an alley and she realises he is going in the direction of We Are One. The electricity stops.

"Let's stay here," she says. "I don't want to go down there."

Zeus looks at her and Jesse thinks she sees a tinge of annoyance in his eyes. He thinks she has changed her mind. Jesse's other half appears on the other side of the road, leaning against a brick wall, arms folded, watching. *Go away. This is nothing to do with you.*

"There's no-one here," she says quickly. "If we go further that way, we'll come to the industrial estate where other kids hang about."

A slow smile spreads over Zeus's face as he pushes her into the wall.

Artemis has been searching for Jesse everywhere. She's not at sixth form, she's not at home, she's not at We Are One. They've hardly spent any time together since she came back and now when Artemis really needs her, she is nowhere to be seen. Artemis sits on a bench in the college grounds, pulling her cardigan round her shoulders as the wind whistles through the trees, watching leaves flutter through the afternoon air and land by her feet. She is still sitting there half an hour later, sighing, worrying, chewing her nails, picking the varnish off them, when Debra struts over. The last person she wants to see right now.

"Room for a little one?" asks Debra, slumping down on the bench and resting her head on Artemis's shoulder before waiting for an answer. "I really need a shoulder to cry on."

That makes two of us, thinks Artemis. But she needs Jesse's shoulder. Artemis folds her arms, hugging herself, wishing she was wearing a coat. Debra's head balances on the bony part of her shoulder, pressing uncomfortably against her and making her arm go numb.

"What's up?" asks Artemis, keeping her tone light.

Debra kicks her feet out, making the leaves rustle. She has a ladder in her opaque, black tights and her shiny, patent pumps are scuffed at the toes. It's not like Debra.

"It's Derek. He's dumped me."

"Oh." Artemis feels Debra's silky hair touch her neck as she moves her head.

"Is that all you can say?" snaps Debra, jerking her head off Artemis's shoulder and sitting bolt upright. "I am devastated and all you can say is 'Oh'!"

"What do you want me to say? I am sorry that Derek

has dumped you." *Lie.* "But you're not the only one with problems, you know. Did he say why? Is he with someone else?"

"He said things were getting too serious." Debra lets out a sigh. "He's not ready for a serious relationship. He needs to be on his own for a while."

"Meaning, he wants to play around," says Artemis, watching Debra's face fall. "Sorry, it's just, you know, that's what it normally means when a boy says that sort of thing to a girl."

The girls stare out at the tree lined road, watching cars drive up and down. Debra looks crestfallen; she bites her lower lip. For a minute, Artemis wishes she hadn't said anything.

"Oh, it's okay. He wasn't all that anyway. And he did make me look fat, the lanky git!" Debra laughs and turns to face Artemis, taking Artemis's hands in hers, inspecting her chipped blue nail varnish. "Girl, you really need a manicure. Come over to mine later and I'll sort these manky hands out. So… what's your problem then? You and Randy are still all right, aren't you?"

Artemis raises her eyebrows and pulls a grimace. *Why does everything have to be so complicated?*

"Uh oh."

When Artemis finally catches up with Jesse later, she is reeling from her exchange with Debra and more than a little nervous about going round to see her.

"Jesse!" she shouts across the street. "There you are! I've been looking for you everywhere. Why weren't you at college?"

Artemis takes in her friend's appearance, the dark circles round her eyes, the dull, greasy hair. Jesse has been transformed since her Gender Assignment, what with her short hair and new look but this is something else. She looks terrible.

"Hey, are you okay?" asks Artemis, crossing the street and placing a hand on Jesse's arm.

"No. I dunno. I couldn't face coming in today. I feel crap about stuff."

Artemis feels hostile vibes and her hand instantly shoots up to her mouth to resume nail chewing. "You know don't you? You hate me, don't you?"

"What are you talking about?"

"Hang on, what are you talking about? What stuff?"

"I can't talk here," says Jesse. "I should go home. I just wanted to get some air to clear my head. Why don't you come back to ours for a bit?"

She doesn't know.

"Come over to mine for a change."

The conversation is stilted as they walk over to the house, as they both skirt round the issues that are worrying them, instead chattering on about homework and bands and the new season's fashions. Once at Artemis's house, they make their way to her bedroom, bypassing her younger sisters squabbling downstairs. Artemis's room is plain but feminine at the same time. The walls are painted a soft lilac, the room minimally furnished, with a white, painted, wooden bed and matching wardrobe and dressing table. Strewn over the dressing table are hairbrushes, perfumes and jewellery.

"So what's up? Why are you feeling crap?" asks Artemis once they have settled down on the bed and cranked some music on.

"I slept with Zeus…" says Jesse, biting her lip.

"Oh. My. God!" exclaims Artemis. "And?! Oh… not good, eh?"

Jesse shakes her head, tears forming in her eyes.

"Oh, hun. It was your first time, right? Everyone's first time is crap. Plus you'd only recently been assigned. Were you even properly healed?"

"I dunno. It wasn't just that. I just… I dunno. I thought everything would be different once I was assigned. That I would be different."

"Well, you look pretty different, you seem pretty different."

"I don't feel different though. Not in the way I thought I would. It hasn't made everything right. Then, I thought if I slept with Zeus it would but…"

"But it hasn't hey? I know what this calls for. Chocolate cake!"

As Artemis heads downstairs for comfort food, Jesse can't stop the images of Zeus coming into her mind.

Her skin prickles as she remembers his hands sliding under her top and unhooking her bra. She liked the fact that he wanted her so much. She felt so desired, so special. A sexy, young woman. She wanted to do it. He was kissing her neck. It felt good. But what if he could tell she wasn't the real thing? Now, his smiling face right in front of her, the weight of his body as he pushes her into the wall. He is gorgeous, right? Her heart is banging like mad as his hands slide inside her knickers. She panics that he'll be able to tell that she has only recently been assigned, will feel her scars, something to give her away, but recalls Dr Shah's words assuring her that it would be very difficult for anyone to tell.

"In any event, it's not that uncommon for those operated on at birth to have further surgery as a teen," she'd said. "Things don't always go strictly to plan in the first operation and of course, the body can change in surprising ways. No-one will be able to tell."

"I really want you, Jesse," he groaned in her ear, taking her hand and pushing it onto his erection.

"It's my first time!" she squeaked and he stopped then, moved his head to look at her.

"I'll be gentle," he murmured.

She watched as he took a condom out of his back pocket and ripped it open, not wanting to tell him that he probably didn't need it, she probably couldn't get pregnant anyway. Nobody knew. She watched as he rolled it on as though it was something he did every day, like cleaning his teeth. It was as though it was happening to someone else.

He couldn't tell. She didn't think he could tell.

Jesse closes her eyes.

Artemis returns with a tray of treats.

"Look, I don't want to talk about things with your brother, you know, I don't want to gross you out but I do understand, you know, about thinking everything will be different once you've had sex. Look, I'm not the best person to advise you, I... I don't know how to tell you this... God, I need a chocolate brownie."

She pauses to stuff the brownie into her mouth in one go.

"So what is it you were talking about earlier?" asks Jesse, picking at a cake on a napkin, turning it round on her lap.

"I've split up with Randy," mumbles Artemis, with her mouth full.

"Oh, I'm sorry. What happened? Did he dump you?"

Artemis shakes her head, trying to swallow the food down.

"Did he do something bad?" Jesse sits upright, leaning forward, seeming eager to listen.

Another head shake, as she takes a sip of milk.

"Did *you* do something bad? Is that why you said that weird stuff earlier about me hating you?"

"I didn't do anything," begins Artemis. "I finished it. Please eat something!"

The tray sits between them, a carnival of calories, everything Ask Alex would advise a girl not to eat if she wanted to get a boy to notice her. Jesse stuffs the cake into her mouth, Artemis style and picks up a giant cookie off of the china plate.

"Okay, so did you have a falling out? Have you just grown apart? Is there someone else?"

At the last question, Artemis puts her head in her hands.

"Promise you won't hate me."

"Oh god, how can I promise that when I don't even know what you've done? Randy's my brother, you know!"

She holds the cookie in the air, starting to feel nauseous.

"I haven't done anything but I do like someone else. I haven't done anything though. You can't help who you fancy, right? I haven't done anything. Don't look at me like that, please, Jesse? I thought you were my friend. I haven't done the dirty on your brother. That's why I finished it. I wouldn't do that to him."

"Anyone I know?"

The cookie crumbles in her hands, leaving a mess of crumbs on Artemis's pretty bed covers.

Artemis nods.

19

The room is filled with the sound of screaming, primal and raw. A woman's cries are joined by a higher, lighter bleating.

"You have a beautiful baby, Julie!" exclaims Ana, holding the newborn out of the water, its face streaked and bruised-looking, just like every other baby that was born before it.

The baby's dark eyes dart around the room, before settling on its mother's face.

"Is it, you know?" says Julie, eyes searching, lighting up and fading again.

"A beautiful baby," repeats Ana. "Time will tell, Julie. Time will tell."

Julie's body sags in the birthing pool, as she clutches the child to her chest.

Jesse paces outside the hall at We Are One, waiting for Ork. She has been waiting for a while and has started to become cold. She shoves her hands into the pockets of her denim jacket, wishing she had something warmer on, a thicker coat, gloves and a scarf. Jordan appears in phers leather jacket, laughing with Hunter, who, for once, is smiling. They are so engrossed in each other that they don't notice Jesse waiting. *When will Ork come out?* As she waits and paces, she thinks about Artemis's revelation and her head hurts. Was Artemis wrongly assigned at birth? Should she have been made into a boy? But Artemis doesn't think that. She says she likes being a girl. It's just that she likes Deb. More than likes Deb. It's too much for Jesse to take in right now. She is a girl and she needs to be with a boy. It is simple, right? So why is she here, lurking in shadows, waiting for Ork?

Phe comes out of the building, zipping up phers jacket, and walks down the metal staircase. And Jesse knows. She knows that she has been fighting feelings that cannot be denied, just like Artemis was fighting her true feelings for Deb.

"Ork!" she calls out.

"Whoa, you nearly gave me a heart attack!" phe laughs. "What are you doing hiding behind bins?"

Jesse notices that Ork's hair has grown a little, phe has to keep pushing phers fringe out of phers eyes. Phe is still wearing the multi coloured scarf. Jesse and Ork wear matching black eye liner.

"I just want to talk. Is everyone gone? Can we go back in the hall and have a hot chocolate? Start that conversation over again?"

"Sure we can go back," says Ork, turning around and going back up the stairs, keys dangling from phers hand.

The stairs creak as they ascend together. Back inside, Jesse can barely see. She waits for Ork to switch on the lights.

"Sorry about the darkness. The electric's been cut. It'll have to be a cold drink, I'm afraid."

"Oh."

Jesse watches as Ork flicks on a lighter and lights a candle on a table by the sofa, moving swiftly until the area is softly lit by six candles. There is an open cardboard box by the side of the sofa. Jesse can see strips of shiny material.

"What's that?" she asks, gesturing to the box.

"That's the We Are One sashes and badges."

Ork pulls a sash out of the box and drapes it over phers leg, fishing about in the bottom of the box before pulling out a clear, polythene bag, full of badges.

"Oh, let's have a look."

Phe unravels the sash and slips it over phers head, pinning a badge onto phers scarf. Both feature yellow, purple, green and white stripes, the words, "Equal Rights for The Third Gender" and a yin and yang symbol with the words, "We Are One" printed across it. Jesse fingers the silky sash.

"They look good," she says, frowning. "What are they for?"

"To convey our message. So, look, what did you want to talk about?" asks Ork, as they sit awkwardly on the sofa.

Phe smiles shyly at Jesse. They have never been alone before.

"The last time I came here, I just to… you seemed so angry at me… I just…"

"I'm sorry I was off with you, Jesse," says Ork, sipping phers drink. "I like you. I thought…"

"I like you too."

Silence except for the swish of Ork's sash against phers shirt.

Jesse puts her hand on Ork's and waits for the electricity to start.

"I really like you."

"Don't, Jesse," says Ork, looking afraid.

But Jesse ignores pherm and moves her hand to phers face, their eyes locked. She moves her face towards phers to kiss pherm. It feels so different than kissing Zeus. Ork's lips are fuller and softer. Phe responds tentatively. This time Jesse feels in control. She opens her mouth and sits astride pherm. Ork stares at her as she slowly removes the sash and unwraps phers scarf.

"Jesse…"

"Shhh, don't talk."

A fox whines out in the street, a sound that cuts to the

bone. Jesse hears the wheelie bins creaking. No doubt they'll be tipped over, their contents spewed out over the pavement. But she doesn't want to think of bins or foxes. She doesn't want to think at all.

In the dark, she cannot see Ork's body but she feels every contour as she undresses pherm. It feels similar to her own body before she had Assignment but different too. Ork sits there, watching Jesse's hands move over pherm. Her body is on fire, as she moves on top of Ork.

"We are one," she whispers.

Ork's eyes shine in the light. At that moment, everything makes sense, everything is real and true and good and lovely. After, they lie in each other's arms for a while until Jesse starts to worry about the time.

"My mum will be wondering where I am," she says into the darkness.

"Oh yeah, your mother," says Ork, shifting slightly so their bodies part.

Jesse cannot read phers voice.

Jesse creeps into the house as quietly as she can, hoping her mother is still out. Ana is home later and later these days, her work at NBM consuming more of her time. As she is tiptoeing down the hall, she hears the key in the lock and quickly kicks off her shoes and throws her jacket into the living room, where it lands on the armchair.

"Hi Mum. I was just going to get a drink. Want one?"

Her mother looks preoccupied, radiant, full of love, just how Jesse feels.

"Oh yes, darling, please. I've just delivered a beautiful, precious new baby into the world. Such a special day, such an honour."

Jesse knows her mother won't be asking too many questions.

That night, Jesse is visited by her other half again. He appears in her dreams, and when she wakes, he stands before her, faded now, sad looking. He kneels before her and takes her hand, resting his forehead on her knuckles. Something about the feel of his skin reminds her of her father. Unable to get back to sleep, she passes the rest of the night, looking into his eyes and trying to understand what he wants her to do. She can think of nothing else the next day, not even Artemis and Deb. Artemis sits in lessons staring out of the window lost in her own thoughts, as Jesse is in hers. Her brain fizzes through to the next night when she finds herself walking back to the hall. She doesn't even know where Ork lives but she has sent a message on her mobile for pherm to meet her there. There is no meeting tonight so she doesn't have to wait for others to leave. The crisp night air crackles, stars burn brightly in the sky. Jesse walks up the creaky stairs and pushes open the door, letting her eyes adjust to the candlelight. When she sees Ork, she rushes over to pherm and takes pherm by the hands. Phe says nothing.

"I need to talk to you," she says.

"We both know what talking turns into." Phe is talking in phers blank voice again. It is hard for Jesse to know what phe is feeling.

"I thought about you all last night," says Jesse, swallowing a lump in her throat. "I'm falling for you. I think I'm falling in love with you." There she has said it.

"Jesse, I… I've got a lot of feelings for you too but I don't see how we can be together."

"Maybe there *is* a way we can be together… if you love me. If you love me as I am now…"

"And what Jesse? Are you going to introduce me to your mother? What as? Your boyfriend? I don't see how it can ever work unless I have Gender Assignment as a boy."

Jesse's heart thumps. One of the candles burns down and flickers out.

"I know it seems hard and yes, it would be so much easier for us to be together if you became a boy. We wouldn't need to hide in places like this. We could…"

Ork drops phers hands and pulls away. "For you to even say that to me! To even suggest! You don't know what love is, Jesse. This is who I am. If you can't accept me for who I am, we might as well forget anything ever happened. In fact, yeah, I think that would be for the best." Ork's voice is cold and dark.

"Then neither do you know what love is! You can't accept me as I am either, can't think of me as anything other than a Half! I know you'd prefer it if I hadn't had Assignment. Just be honest, you would. Wouldn't you?"

"Yes, I would. I never pretended to agree with your decision to have Assignment. Hunter told me I should try to stop you but I didn't think it was my place. You had to do what you felt was right for you."

"And it is right for me. It is! I think you're just afraid. But if you go through with it, you'll feel so much better afterwards."

"Is that what you feel? So much better? Is that why you're going around shagging anything that moves?!"

A slap in the face. *How does phe know?*

"That, that prick has been mouthing off to everyone about doing it with you in the alley! I heard him telling someone in the supermarket, going into all the details of what you did, what you were like. Half the world knows about you sleeping together! Think he cares about you? You were just a conquest."

"I'm sorry you had to hear that." Jesse speaks quietly,

tears pricking in her eyes, sick rising in her throat.

"Sorry you did it or just sorry I found out?"

"Zeus was a mistake. It was before we… That was my first time. It, it was just me trying to prove I was a girl… It's different with you, I…"

Tears stream down her face now but Ork's face remains frozen.

"You could have it reversed you know, but I wouldn't ask you to do that. You are who you are and I am who I am. Maybe what happened between *us* was a mistake too. I think you should go."

20

In a house in the middle of nowhere, babies wrapped in khaki coloured blankets sleep in their cribs, toddlers in chocolate brown playsuits run about collapsing on their bottoms and parents try their best to raise their children without gender, just like Ana had done with Jesse and Randy years before. The door opens and a woman with a pale face, wearing a turquoise tie-dye dress and a long string of amber beads opens it to be confronted by men and women with ID cards.

"Can we come in please, madam?"

The woman hesitates, shuffling her bare feet, in contrast to the still, shiny, black patent boots of the officials, rooted firmly to the ground.

"We have reason to believe that this house is the site of criminal activity."

The sound of movement from behind her. Curtains swish. A baby cries a shrill, piercing cry.

"We have reason to believe that there are children in this house who have not had Compulsory Gender Assignment, madam."

The woman is shaking her head. She is rubbing her arms as though she is freezing.

"We need to come and see the children, madam."

Her feeble arms attempt to block the officials, as she pushes the door shut. A firm hand pushes back.

"You have to let us in. We have warrants."

Ork has been working through the night to get the campaign under way. Letters and petitions are all very well but they don't make people sit up and listen, don't force people to listen. No. Militant action is what's needed. Things cannot go on as they are. Something has to change. Phe taps phers fingers on the table, phers knee trembling. Something has to give.

"It's time to take drastic action," phe says to the assembled group. "It's time to pursue extreme measures of civil disobedience."

"I agree," says Max, nodding towards phers sibling. Phe has shaved the underside of phers head now and wears the top half up in a ponytail of bright purple hair.

"Yeah, I've been saying that for ages," chips in Hunter, sitting cross-legged on the floor holding Jordan's hand in phers lap. "The only thing the world listens to these days is terrorism. How about letter bombs to start? We could target all the sour faced politicians who rant on about the evils of intersex. How about that guy who came up with The Gender Assignment Act for starters. Let's blast him off the face of the planet and see how he likes being targeted for a change."

Ork looks at pherm. "Shut up!"

Jordan removes phers hand from Hunter's grip and stands up.

"We're not going to hurt anyone, except maybe ourselves, for those of you who are willing to step up to the plate and show what you believe in."

"What do you mean?" asks Jordan.

"Count me in," says Max.

"We need to go public, simple as that," says Ork.

"But we can't," whispers Jordan. "What will they do to us?"

"People know we exist anyway," says Hunter. "They choose to turn a blind eye. They don't want to acknowledge who we are."

"But we'll make them acknowledge us, right?" says Max, looking at Ork. "We'll make people understand who we are."

Ork rises from phers seat and paces the room, phers face transformed, determined. "They won't be able to turn a blind eye, then. We'll make them see us."

"They'll lock us up for inciting crime!" urges Jordan, gripping Ork's arm. "They'll put the young ones into detention centres, force counselling on them to brainwash them, put them into rehab and spit them out as Halves!"

"I'll volunteer to lead by example," says Ork.

"We'll do it together," says Max. "We Are One."

Ana puts down the phone and sits in her car staring ahead, shaking. She opens the car door and vomits on the gravel path.

Jesse had been worrying about how to avoid Zeus after they slept together, worrying about how to get out of another date, agonising over whether or not to tell him the truth, whether to dump him without explanation. She need not have worried. He hasn't phoned, hasn't messaged her, hasn't called round to see her, standing on the doorstep with a goofy grin and flexed muscles. He hasn't done any of those things. He hasn't, in fact, made one ounce of an effort to contact her again. After what Ork had told her about Zeus mouthing off to his mates about having sex with her, she doesn't know why she should be surprised. But boys do that, right? They brag to their mates about sex but it doesn't always mean they don't like you, does it?
"Do you think it's because I didn't do it right?" she asks Artemis, rubbing her mascara-streaked cheeks, as they sit cross-legged on Artemis's white painted wooden bed, the cut-out heart in the headboard mocking her. "Is that why he hasn't called? Do you think it's because I wasn't good enough?"

"Don't be ridiculous, Jesse," says Artemis, hugging

her friend and passing her tissues. "It's because he's an arse hole. I'm sorry to say it but it's like he got what he wanted from you and now he doesn't want to know. That's what most boys are like. And they say the Nine Per Cent are the worst of all."

"B-but why do they d-do that?" Jesse blows her nose loudly.

She knows she is crying for Ork not Zeus but somehow the conversation she is having with Artemis right now seems a whole lot easier than the one they should be having.

"I don't even care about him," mutters Jesse, looking up at Artemis out of the corner of her eye, waiting for her reaction.

"It's okay if you do, Jesse. I know you liked him. We've all been there, hun. But nobody likes to be used, do they?"

Jesse thinks about Ork. She can't bear thinking about pherm.

"Have you said anything to Debra yet?" she asks, trying to steer the attention away from herself.

"Oh for God's sake NO and I don't ever intend to!" retorts Artemis, playing with a piece of loose cotton at the end of her fraying jeans. "It's destined to be unrequited love. Maybe that's the best way. Never get your heart broken that way. Anyway, what's the point when she's straight?"

"Maybe she's bi. Things aren't always what they seem…"

"Debra? Bi? I can't see it somehow. Maybe that's why I like her. Maybe it's all about self-protection."

"Artemis," says Jesse, not wanting to keep up the pretence with her best friend. "There's something I need to tell you about Ork and me…"

When Jesse and Artemis get to We Are One's meeting place, there is nobody there except Jordan, blowing out the candles.

"They've gone over to the town hall. Max, Ork and the others," says Jordan, right eye twitching.

"Come on, Jesse. You really need to talk to Ork."

"I didn't agree with any of it," says Jordan, as the last flame is extinguished. "I just wanted to help people."

"With what?" asks Artemis. "You didn't agree with what?"

As the bus turns into the main road forty-five minutes later, they can see the fire blazing, orange and angry, shooting flames up into the air. It licks the night air, black smoke swirling out of control above it, as it creeps higher and higher.

"Oh my God," whispers Jesse, blood pumping ferociously round her body, as she strains her neck to get a better view out of the top deck window.

She has never seen anything like it. The only fires she has seen in real life are the small, managed kind that grown-ups organise on bonfire night, fires that take ages to get going and burn out before the sparklers and rockets have finished fizzing, before the chestnuts and jacket potatoes have been eaten. But this fire does not look like it will burn out at all. This fire looks like the fires from people's nightmares, the fires from the depths of hell, like it will burn for all eternity. Jesse can make out Hunter and Rowan and some of the others from the crowds. As they get off the bus and walk towards the scene, Jesse sees that they are wearing the sashes. Yellow, purple, green and white stripes. Rowan has a knife and is holding a plastic doll in phers hand, cutting it into pieces and tossing it into the flames, until all that's left is a head. Hunter is holding up a certificate.

"Here's what I think to my Gender Assignment Certificate!" phe shouts, ripping it into shreds and throwing the pieces, watching them flutter and burn. "We say NO to Compulsory Gender Assignment! We say NO to…"

But, wait… Ork is not there. Jesse's erratic pulse starts to calm down. Phe's not here. She knew phe wouldn't do anything like this. She can't see Max either. They must have chased after Hunter and Rowan and the other trouble makers, tried to make them see sense, tried to talk them out of anything foolish. Jesse thinks back to the box of sashes and badges, the image of Ork slipping one on proudly. She never did find out what they were for. Were they for this all along? Why hadn't phe told her what they were planning?

"Let's go. It's not safe!" calls Artemis, as the flames grow in size, threatening to destruct the entire town.

"Wait!" cries Jesse. "I need to see."

Artemis pulls Jesse away, but she turns back to watch the fire burn, the crowds growing, the sound of sirens wailing now. Artemis is dragging her faster now, away from the chaos, hurting Jesse's arm. Her eyes are everywhere. Phe isn't here. It's okay. She can talk to Ork in a few days when things have calmed down. Maybe it will even make pherm want to leave the group.

And then, by the side entrance of the town hall, Jesse sees Max, chained to the railings, dressed in purple harem pants and a yellow tee-shirt, a white and green checked scarf round phers neck, the badge pinned to the scarf, the sash proudly displayed across phers chest. Phers hands are holding one side of a huge banner. "We Are One wants Equal Rights for The Third Gender." And holding the other side is Ork.

21

Jesse reads every article, watches every report, sits glued to the news channel 24-7. *They are a threat to society and should be kept behind bars,* one newspaper says. The prime minister delivers a speech about the feral underclass threatening to destroy civilised society. *They aren't like you or me. They are dangerous. They need to be dealt with.* Jesse stares at the tabloid headline: *Suffragender riots!* A picture of Emmeline Pankhurst wearing her suffragette uniform and brooch appears next to a picture of Ork and Max chained to the railings wearing their sashes and badges. Inside a small photograph of Ork and Max at the commune, Max wearing the pink bracelet, phers face covered in freckles. Where had they got it from?

"Jesse?" Ana stares at her daughter, sat hunched over a newspaper at the breakfast table. "Artemis rang? Are you going to call her back?"

"Maybe later," says Jesse, pouring over the pages.

It wasn't just their town where trouble had broken out. Everywhere up and down the country, members of We Are One were taking action. Some chained themselves to railings like Ork and Max, others disrupted official meetings. There was an unprecedented number of arrests. Papers and the official government websites (which were about the only websites allowed in this era of policed Internet activity) published photos of suspects with phone numbers to report their whereabouts. Courts were working round the clock to process the trials with a quick turnaround. Some were fined, others sent straight to prison. Just as Jordan had predicted, under age members were sent to detention centres, forced into rehab. People started smashing windows. There were arson attacks. They entered schools and sabotaged Male and Female Life Skills lessons, destroying equipment and burning books. Hospitals and the medics who carried out Gender Assignment Surgery received letter bombs and death threats. An anonymous statement sent to the papers from We Are One said that they did not condone these acts of violence. They were peaceful protesters. But violence ensued all the same. The prisons were filling up. Ork and Max were given five years in prison each for the crime of inciting a riot and breach of the peace. Rowan and Hunter got three years. *They were a threat to society. They had to be stopped. Nobody knew how many intersex people were left roaming the streets.*

"Jesse? Are you going into college today? Shall I run you a bath?"

Jesse's eyes are vacant as she stares back at her mother. "What did you say?"

"You haven't eaten your breakfast again, sweetheart," says Ana, sitting next to Jesse and placing her hands on her shoulders, casually looking down at the thick wad of papers that Jesse is scanning. "Please have some toast. Then let me run you a bath. You need to get back to normal, darling."

"Normal?" says Jesse, slowly, rolling the word around in her mouth. "What's normal? People are saying my friends are perverted and evil. Is that normal? What's normal?"

She looks back at the page, pushing the toast away.

"No, no. I understand how you feel. They're not, not evil..." Ana seizes the moment, grabs Jesse's hands. "They need our compassion, yes, they need our help, they were damaged, you see. It's not their fault they were denied Gender Assignment and left this way. It's their parents' fault. Look."

She points to a headline: *Stolen childhoods.*

"See it says here that your friends need support and education, don't they? They need medical help, a gradual re-integration back into normal society."

"Normal?"

Jesse stands up and switches on the television. The prime minister's face fills the screen, his enormous quiff bouncing as he booms, "We will hunt you down. We will find you."

She falls back onto the sofa, pressing the remote control. Another channel shows mug shots of those arrested. A drug addict, a law student and a teaching assistant. Neighbours appear on daytime television, done up to the nines, eagerly gossiping about the stranger next door. *I had no idea I was living next to one of them. He seemed like an ordinary bloke, but he wasn't was he? Wasn't even a bloke at all.*

Flick. Flick. Flick. Every channel is the same. Members of the elite Nine Per Cent host debates and chatshows. A female celebrity pushes her new clothing line with the slogan, "100 Per Cent Female".

"Jesse?"

Flick. Flick. Flick. A TV chef flashes his book on foods to balance the hormones, with different diets for men and women and a special food programme for babies and children. Jesse realises for the first time that all those in power are of that kind. There are no MPs who don't belong to the Nine Per Cent. The elite few are running the country, up on their pedestals of gender perfection.

"Jesse? You really should think about going back to college."

Jesse stands up. "I'm going out."

"Good," says Ana, her shoulders relaxing. "That's good. Shall I run you a bath?"

Jesse pushes past her mother and walks out the door, still wearing her pyjamas. She goes to the newsagents, thumbing the glossy magazines with their sensationalised coverage: graphic images of intersex bodies, details of the sex practices of ambigendered people. Jesse wonders where it will end. The Nine Per Cent are safe. People like Zeus and Deb would never have to worry. Those who had their Compulsory Gender Assignment at birth would be okay too. They would never be leaders, never make the laws, or determine the future of the next generation but they would be okay. They wouldn't have to live in fear. But what about girls and boys like her, whose parents had broken the law, who had been raised neither male nor female, who had only been assigned as teens? Would they be slapped with Compulsory Rehabilitation Treatment Orders too?

She can't get the image of Ork's face out of her head, the look of contempt that phe gave her as she stood before pherm and Max by the town hall. She had looked at him through the blur of her tears, unable to speak, unable to think, until Artemis had pulled her away. Why hadn't she said anything to pherm? Now phe would hate her for sure.

22

One day you are wondering how the earth can go on turning, how people can get out of bed in the morning and put on their clothes and go to school and work as though nothing has happened, can sit at desks in skirts and suits eating cheese sandwiches and drinking tea and doing normal, everyday things. Then the next day, you are doing the same, getting dressed and eating muesli for breakfast and putting your college work in your bag and heading out the door. Jesse and Artemis are back in class, wearing lipstick and mascara, talking about fashion and music, buying chip butties at lunchtime and reading gossip magazines. But things aren't the same.

There are police on the streets. There is security all over the college. Students whose fingerprints don't match the computer records and those without their ID cards on them are being refused entry. Guards patrol the gate and grounds, eyes searing. The sound of teen banter is replaced by the drone of walkie talkies. Teachers have creases in their foreheads and get called into special meetings at the end of classes. Syllabuses are being reviewed and revised. Everything is changing.

"I'm sorry about Deb," says Jesse, through a mouthful of butty, mayonnaise dripping down her chin.

Artemis shrugs, handing Jesse a serviette. "Yuk, wipe your chin, girl! Ditto Zeus. Who would have thought those two would get together?"

"Well, I guess it makes sense. They are both members of the Nine Per Cent club after all. Haven't you noticed that they are all sticking to their own kind now? Everyone is so suspicious."

After college, Jesse says goodbye to Artemis and makes her way home. As she rounds the corner to her maisonette, she is taken aback by the sight of paparazzi exploding outside her house. There are hoards of them, holding up big, imposing cameras, eyes trained on the front door to her home. A pack of wolves waiting to pounce on their prey. Her heart pounds. Standing by the oak tree on the corner, she reels back, unsure what to do – turn and run far away from these predators or attempt to burst through them to reach her home, her family. A short, fat, balding man holding a camera is kneeling at the door and shouting through the letterbox.

"How do you feel knowing your daughter was taught by one of them?"

The curtains are drawn. Jesse pulls her phone out of her pocket. A missed call from her mother. Ana never allows closed curtains during daylight, always whips them open first thing every morning, says it's important to let the light in. Bright light. A flash goes off in Jesse's face, momentarily blinding her. Someone is in front of her, another beside her, behind her. She is cornered. She cannot breathe.

"Jesse! Jesse!"

The next day a picture of a pale, wide-eyed looking Jesse appears in the paper, along with the caption, *Shocked response of girl taught by Mrs P.* Jesse sees Mrs Pritchard at the front of the classroom from her old school, her eyes staring out from the page. The prime minister is on TV again, his face even greyer than usual.

"We are only now beginning to be able to assess the scale of the problem. We do not yet know how many people have not been corrected at birth but new intelligence is coming in on a daily basis. It is not just the innocent babies who have to pay the consequences for their parents neglecting to have their birth defects cured as some kind of misguided social experiment. It is the whole society that must now face the burden of these consequences. And face it head on is exactly what we must do, what we will do. You have my utmost reassurance on that."

More and more pictures of Ork are appearing in the news since phe has been sentenced for inciting criminal behaviour. Phe is being singled out as a ringleader. New articles appear on a daily basis. Coverage is exploding. Jesse prefers to watch the news when she is alone in the house, or take the newspapers up to her room to pour over in solitude. She sits on the edge of her bed now, papers spilling out of her rucksack, her fingers tracing the outline of Ork's face in yet another double page spread. There is a photo of pherm smiling at the camera in happier times, looking beautiful, looking like the Ork she remembers from their very first meeting, all full lips and dark eyes. The same picture appears in all the papers with different headlines. *The Poster Boy-girl of Intersex. The Face of the Third Gender. The Teen Who Led a Nation to Riot.*

Jesse's hand flies to her mouth at the latest report. *Political Prisoner or Just Another Hooligan?* The story claims that Ork is fighting back with a hunger strike, getting thinner and weaker day by day. There is a quote by a medical doctor explaining what happens when someone does not eat. After three days, the liver starts processing body fat, in a process called ketosis. After three weeks, the body enters starvation mode where it mines muscles and vital organs for energy, and loss of bone marrow becomes life-threatening. Jesse wretches.

The front door slams and Jesse stuffs the papers back down in her ruck sack.

"Yeah, it was a great match mate!" Her brother, Randy's voice.

They haven't spoken much in recent weeks. Not since Artemis dumped Randy and Zeus dumped Jesse, albeit by omission. At least Artemis had the decency to talk to Randy.

"You're joking. It was crap!"

Zeus.

He hasn't been round since. But obviously he and Randy are mates. She can't expect Randy not to see his friend any more, just as he shouldn't expect her not to continue her friendship with Artemis, although she knows he's not happy about it. He storms out of the room whenever she's on the phone to her or mentions her name. The sound of Zeus's voice now makes her feel shaky. They haven't had any closure. The last time she saw or spoke to him was when he was pushing her against a wall, doing things to her she'd never done with anyone before. She was pretty sure he couldn't tell that she'd only recently been assigned. Surely if he'd had any idea he would have blagged about it to all his mates. She can see now that that is precisely the type of lad he is, hasn't a clue why she even fancied him before. She wonders if Randy feels nervous like her, nervous that his secret will be discovered too. Okay, so they are assigned now, but their mother still broke the law in opting out of Gender Assignment at birth and leaving them until their teens to have surgery.

"Did you hear about old Mackie from the chippy?" bellows Zeus.

Jesse hadn't noticed before that his voice was so loud.

"What about him?"

Jesse can detect nerves in the rise of Randy's voice.

"He's only one of them lot who had nutters for parents, isn't he? Left him as a no mark freak until he reached puberty and they thought they better do something about it. Probably had him dressed up in a frilly tutu doing ballet and playing with dolls at home half the time or something.

I can't even imagine it, can you, having girlie bits down there an all! Might be interesting to play with yourself, I guess!"

Randy is laughing really hard and then changes the subject, asking about how things are going with Deb. Jesse tries to shut her ears as Zeus recounts in lurid detail all the things they've been up to together in Deb's bedroom, while her folks have been out. She tunes out, imagining Ork's voice. *Jesse, I... I've got a lot of feelings for you too but I don't see how we can be together.* Picturing phers face when she kissed pherm for the first time, the startled look that gripped phers featured and then softened. And then that day by the railings…

"She's amazing, Deb is. A really amazing girl. I mean I'm sorry it didn't work out with your sister and everything. Obviously, she's a great girl too. But Deb, she's just got the most amazing…"

Jesse sits back down on her bed and switches the radio on to drown out the sound of Zeus's voice.

23

The next morning, the police are at the door. Drumming at the door. Jesse is still in bed.

The night before, Ana sat her two children down and told them that they were going to stay put. Earlier plans for moving were on hold.

"I know Maya thinks we should move away but I think we should stay where we are for now. If we take you out of education and move home again, it will only arouse suspicion. We're suspending work at Natural Souls, just for a while until all this madness dies down. Things are not safe at the moment."

"So what about the pregnant women that are just about to have their babies, the women who need you? They can't just suspend birth can they?" says Randy, leaning back in his chair, smirking.

He is so different these days, has acquired a hard edge. If this is what it means to be a 'proper teenage boy', Jesse thinks she can do without proper boys. She sits quietly. She had forgotten Ana's plans to move. All she can think about is Ork.

While Zeus went on about Debra's assets, Jesse went online to try to find out if there was any more information on Ork's hunger strike, knowing that the official websites would present a skewed view of phers plight. The websites simply said that phe was a convicted criminal who was engaging in self-harm. But out on the street, things were different. Jesse quietly slid out of the side door of the maisonette to get some air. There was paper all over the road, fluttering in the wind, pages being separated and hurled about. She stopped to pick one up and look at it. A leaflet run off on someone's home computer, hastily put together. "We Are One" was printed at the top and underneath in black and white were the publicly stated goals of Ork's fast:

- All Third Gender protesters detained under the Prevention of Terrorism Act should be released.

- All parents detained for failure to comply with Compulsory Gender Assignment under The Gender Assignment Act should be released.

- The Gender Assignment Act should be abolished.

- Genital mutilation under the guise of Compulsory Gender Assignment should be outlawed.

- Gender Assignment Certificates should be replaced with Birth Certificates, with three categories of sex: Male, Female, and Intersex.

On the next page, a picture of Ork and the quotation, "One day, Third Gender People will be free to live as themselves without fear of persecution. It is a great honour to be able to be part of the solution, fulfilling my personal responsibility to humankind."

The drumming gets louder. Jesse checks her bedside clock. 6am. This can only mean one thing, a dawn raid. Her mother appears in her bedroom doorway, fully dressed, hair neatly groomed, as though she has been waiting for them.

"Jesse, darling," she says kneeling down beside her daughter. "The police are here. We knew this day would come but I promise it will be okay. Don't say anything to them, darling. Leave everything to me."

Then the sound of Ana opening Randy's door, murmured voices as she repeats promises she has no idea whether she can keep.

Jesse listens as her mother opens the door and talks

with the officers, all the while scrambling to get dressed. She hears the change in the tone of her mother's voice and then Ana reappears in the doorway.

"They want to talk to you," she says, her eyebrows joining, her face flushed.

"I thought you said I didn't have to speak to them."

"It's not about us. It's not about Natural Souls or about you not having Gender Assignment as babies," she whispers. "It's about Ork."

"What about Ork?" says Jesse, her heart falling to the floor.

Phe's dead! Phe's dead! Her mind races as she pictures pherm in prison, on a cold, grey slab, dark eyes staring lifelessly at the ceiling, phers full lips blue, phers face drained of all colour. She grabs hold of the door frame for support, her legs threatening to give way under her.

"They're investigating possible sex offences. They've had an anonymous phone call to say that you were raped by Ork."

"W-hat?!" gasps Jesse, doing up her shirt buttons. "That's not true!"

"Thank God," says Ana, her face still in shock. "I knew you would have come to me if anything awful had happened to you."

"I wanted to sleep with Ork. I love pherm!"

"Madam!" calls the officer from the hallway.

"Jesse," whispers Ana, hear hands flying to her cheeks. "I thought you'd stopped seeing those people. You can't tell the police that you were involved with Ork! They'll take you in for questioning. They'll interrogate you. They'll find out everything about you, Randy, me, and Natural Souls."

Jesse takes a deep breath and steps out into the hallway. Randy is waiting, his eyes glowing. It was Randy, she thinks. Randy told the police. *But how did he know about Ork? Did Artemis tell him about Ork? Why would he do it? To get back at me for Artemis dumping him, like it was my fault?*

"We need to ask you some difficult questions, my love," says the female officer, her radio crackling. "Is there somewhere private we can talk?"

"She's only sixteen!" interjects Ana. "I'll stay with her."

"Do you want your mum to sit with you, Jesse? Or would you rather talk to us in confidence? It's up to you. My name's Sharon, by the way."

Jesse looks at her mother. There are things she doesn't want her mother to hear but she is frightened, so terribly frightened. She needs her. Once they are settled in the lounge, teas have been made and Randy has been ushered away, they start to talk.

"We've had an anonymous call that Ork raped you. Do you know anything about that call?"

Jesse shakes her head.

"We would like to arrange to take you to the rape unit to speak to a counsellor there and have an examination."

"I wasn't raped," says Jesse. "It's a lie."

"I understand this must be very hard, Jesse," says Sharon, lifting her cup of tea to her mouth and burning her lips.

"It's a lie."

"Okay, let's start again," says Sharon, returning the cup to its saucer. "Do you know Ork?"

Jesse looks at her mother. There is no point lying about knowing pherm. It will only make it worse. Something must have told the police. Her head is spinning. How much should she say?

"Have you had sexual relations with Ork?"

Jesse looks at her mother again. She nods.

"Did you consent to sexual relations?"

Nod.

"Were you in any way coerced or pressurised into consenting?"

"No, not at all. It was my idea."

Ana looks down at her hands and starts picking her nails, like a child.

Sharon looks from Jesse to Ana and hesitates before speaking.

"Jesse, we understand that these things can be very complicated. Sometimes it can feel as though you are agreeing to something when someone has spent a long time confusing you, working on you, grooming you. These people can be very convincing, very persuasive…"

"No! It wasn't like that. It wasn't like that, at all."

"Okay, okay." Sharon sips her tea and observes Jesse.

Jesse waits for her to speak again.

"So, tell me how you first met Ork."

Jesse tells Sharon about Artemis and how she introduced her to Ork. *Artemis won't get in trouble though, will she?* She hasn't broken any laws and it's not even as though she's got any secrets to hide, well apart from fancying girls. She had Gender Assignment at birth. *They won't be interested in her, will they?* She tells Sharon that they met up in different places, like the street or the park, taking care not to say anything about We Are One or going along to the meetings. She must contact Artemis and let her know what is happening in case she is questioned. She tells her they started seeing each other.

"And you never brought Ork home or introduced this person to your friends or family? Why is that?"

"I knew Ork was different. I didn't think they'd approve."

Sharon nods. "Were you involved in a group called We Are One?"

"No, I wasn't," says Jesse, without missing a beat.

It's the truth, she reminds herself. She was never really involved, never really belonged.

"Did you ever attend any meetings led by Ork?"

"No." A lie.

Is there such a thing as a good lie?

When Jesse has finished her edited account of what happened, Sharon says, "We'll need Artemis's address please to verify some of this information."

She stands up as if to leave and Jesse breathes a sigh of relief.

"Oh and one other thing as a matter of routine," says Sharon, looking from Jesse to Ana and back again, smiling, a bright, tight smile. "We'll just need to see your Gender Assignment Certificates before we go." Sharon turns her attention to Ana, looking at her for the longest time. "And your son's please. That won't be a problem, will it, madam?"

24

Ork sits in phers cell, sweat pricking phers forehead, eyes closed, turning the opened envelope over and over. Phe brings the paper to his face and inhales. Lavender. An unmistakable trade mark. Phe thumbs the torn edges, knowing full well that it wouldn't get past someone like Dumb Douncey or Mad McColgan without being read first. They say letters are only opened to stop people sending in banned stuff, otherwise how simple would it be to send drugs or a knife? They say that nobody reads them, that they are private. Yeah right...

Dear Ork,

    I had to write to you because I really regret the way our last meeting went and I wanted to say sorry. I want you to know that I do accept you as you are and that it was true what I said when I last saw you properly, that I was falling in love with you. Actually, I have fallen in love with you. Every time I see your face in the papers or on the news I wish I could see you. I' m sorry that we couldn' t talk that night when I saw you outside the town hall. I didn' t understand what was going on and I was frightened. I' ve been thinking a lot about everything you have ever said. Your words keep going round in my head day and night and even though I am still confused about some things, I do

believe that there should be equal rights
for intersex people and that people
shouldn't have to have Gender Assignment
surgery if they don't want to. But I also
believe that if people do want to then
they shouldn't be made to feel as though
they are only half a person. I wish we
could all just respect each other's
differences and our choices even if we
don't agree with them. I know it's not
that simple and everything's really
complicated but I can't really say much
more because I don't know who is reading
it or what they might do if I say certain
things but stuff has been pretty difficult
round here since you left. That's a
stupid thing to say, I know, because I
know that nothing I am going through could
compare to the hell you must be going
through in prison.

PLEASE PLEASE PLEASE PLEASE do not
starve yourself. I don't even know if
it's true but that's what all the papers
are saying and I read the We Are One
leaflets that said that you are on a
hunger strike and why you are doing it. I
understand the reasons but I don't want
you to die. I hope you have started eating
again because I read in the paper that
your body will go into starvation mode

within three weeks and it can be life
threatening. Please don' t starve
yourself. Please don' t die. There has to
be another way. I don' t know if you are
still not eating or not because people are
saying a lot of things that I know are
lies. I need you to know that I know they
are lies. If you are starving, I know it
is because you believe in the cause and
you want to make a change for the better
but I can' t bear to think of you
suffering, getting thinner and weaker.
Don' t let them do this to you. It' s not
worth it. There has to be another way to
change things.

I will always love you because you have
taught me a lot. I hope that I have taught
you something too. If you still do have
any feelings for me whatsoever, or even if
you think you might have, please let me
visit so we can talk.

I really really need to see you again.

Please write back.
Love
Jesse xxx

Dear Jesse,

*Thank you for your letter. It means a lot to me. I
guess we both said some things that we didn't mean*

the last time we spoke. It is true that I am on a hunger strike. It's the only real way to protest in prison. I don't know what will happen but I know there is no turning back now. If I die and if my death makes a difference to future generations, it will be worth it. I wouldn't want any children of mine to have to grow up in a world so intolerant, so discriminatory, so evil that they would be damned from the moment they were born, just for being themselves.

If you want to come and see me one last time to say goodbye, then that would help me to make my peace. There is a visiting order and some information attached about arranging the visit.

Love Ork

No kisses. But love all the same. Jesse stares at the letter for the longest time, expecting to cry but instead just staring numbly at the words on the page.

...if I die...

...one last time to say goodbye...

Nothing makes sense any more.

25

Jesse and Artemis take the bus to the prison together and walk to the entrance. They say very little to one another throughout the journey but every few minutes, Artemis offers Jesse a packet of sweets, or a roll of mints or a drink, from her rucksack. Jesse knows it is her way of showing she cares. Artemis kept to Jesse's version of events when the police called and for now, everything seems to be okay. The authorities don't seem to be investigating Jesse's family any further or the ridiculous rape claim.

"Go on, you'll be fine. Say hello from me," calls Artemis, as they part at the entrance. "I'll wait here for you."

It is colder now and Artemis wears thick brown boots and a bright woolly jumper under her denim jacket. Jesse wishes she was wearing the same outfit. She walks inside, keeping her eyes to the ground and trying to keep her breathing steady. At the desk, she hands over the visiting order, her identity card, remembering the struggles her mother had to go through to obtain them and panicking over whether there is anything dodgy looking about the papers, just as she'd panicked when Sharon asked to see their Gender Assignment Certificates. They had them, of course they had them. These things were necessary, required for so many things, like enrolling at school. Ana arranged a fake one for both her children many years ago when they first started school. Dr Shah has written a real one after the op, with a backdated date of entry. The prison officer, a hairy, red-faced man in his fifties, stares at Jesse's papers for a long time, then looks up and stares at her. She smiles tightly and wishes she wasn't wearing make-up. She really didn't know how to present herself today. How are you supposed to visit someone in prison?

It's not something that normally crops up in conversation, not something you can ask your friends or your mum about, is it? And it's certainly not something that's covered on the Female Life Skills Syllabus. In the end, she opted for something smart casual, navy trousers and a white shirt with a blue suede jacket. She almost feels like she's back in school uniform.

The prison officer nods at her and directs her attention to a long list of prohibited items that must not be taken in to give to prisoners. Food is not allowed. The heart shaped box of chocolates burns a hole in her bag. It is a stupid present, anyway. She should never have brought it. It would only seem to be mocking Ork and not respecting phers hunger strike. But how can she respect it? How can she respect something that will lead to phers death? She is asked to leave her bag, phone and any other possessions in a locker in the prison's visitors' area. A female prison officer with frizzy, auburn hair searches her, frisking her legs and arms and checking her pockets. Jesse feels her face go bright red. She could never have come here if she hadn't been assigned. They would have found out straight away and probably thrown her in a cell too.

Jesse is taken through a long, dark corridor by the female prison officer, whose huge bunch of keys jangle as she walks. There are many doors to go through and each one seems to require a different key. No words are spoken as they walk. The corridor smells of an unknown aroma. Jesse can hear far away sounds of shouting and crying, echoing off the walls. Finally, they arrive at the prison 'visits room', set out with chairs and tables with dividing screens separating prisoners from visitors. The officer shows Jesse to the table and then stands in the back of the room, pretending not to watch.

Now the tears come as Ork appears before her, painfully thin, phers eyes huge against phers gaunt face.

"Don't cry, Jesse," phe says, pressing a hand on the screen that separates them.

Jesse puts her hand up to the glass and she cannot contain herself. Out it all comes, the upset, the anger, the fear, the love, pouring, streaming out of her in uncontrollable tears.

"I'm sorry," she says when she finally gets herself under control and feels able to speak again. "I'm so sorry. Please…"

She doesn't know what to say to Ork. She thought everything would be okay if she just saw pherm. She could make it okay. Love would conquer all. But as she faces pherm now she hasn't a clue what to do.

"Jesse," croaks Ork but it seems phe doesn't know what to say either.

Jesse's vision blurs through her tears and as she looks at Ork through the glass barrier, phers image blends into her own reflection. For the first time since Jesse had sex with Zeus, he is back. Her other half.

Then the questions come tumbling out. "Can I do anything for you? Is your solicitor trying to get you out? Are they appealing? What's going on? Do your parents know you and Max are here? Has anyone been to see you?"

"Slow down, Jesse. One question at a time."

"Please don't starve yourself." whines Jesse, unable to contain herself. "Please don't die!"

Ork doesn't speak. Phers eyes are dark and hollow. Phers skin is stretched tight. When phe finally speaks, phe says, "That's not a question." And lets out a hollow laugh.

Jesse wipes her tears away with her sleeve, forcing herself to smile.

"Is your solicitor trying to get you out? Are they appealing?"

"That's two questions. I said one at a time." Ork is smiling at her now, the heat from phers hand palpable through the screen. "The law is not on my side."

"What does that mean? Will there be an appeal?"

"Not within my lifetime," says Ork, looking down.

"But it could be within your lifetime if you eat. You could live for another sixty years, maybe more. You could live to see change. Don't you want to do that, to see change?"

Ork looks at her and she feels phers eyes burn into her like they had when they made love.

"A hunger strike is the only way to protest in here. If I don't protest, then what? What do you think is going to happen to me if I eat and serve out my five years? What do you think is going to happen to me during and after that time? Do you think I'm going to be left in peace? You've no idea what the prison officers are like." Phe is whispering now, angry, hushed tones, eyes flicking up to the frizzy haired woman at the door, who has stopped paying attention and is picking a scab on her elbow. "You've no idea how twisted some of them are, the things they do to prisoners. I'd be better off dead than spend five years in here."

"Five years will go quickly!" gushes Jesse, realising it is a stupid thing to say but feeling desperate. "You might get out quicker. You might be freed. You don't know."

"And after? What do you think will happen? Do you think I'm just going to be released and allowed to carry on with my life as a Third Gender person? I don't know what world you're living in Jesse but if it exists I wish I could live in it with you…"

"You can live in it with me. Let me help you." Jesse

leans into the screen, puts her other hand on it too. Leans her forehead against it, willing Ork to do the same. She cannot bear it, not being able to touch pherm. "Let me help get you out. Can you give me your solicitor's details?"

"Have the police been to see you yet?"

Ork stays seated, calm, in control, one hand on the table.

"Yes, it's okay."

"You want to help me? You want to campaign for me?"

Jesse doesn't speak.

"Do you know what will happen to you, to your family if you try to help me? Are you ready for that?"

"I…"

"Has your mum been arrested yet?"

"No, I…"

"Jesse, I'm tired now. I can't talk for much longer."

Ork's hand starts slipping down the screen.

"I think I have to go now. Take care of yourself, Jesse."

"What can I do? Is there anything else I can do?"

"You could visit Max and tell pherm I love pherm. I don't know if phe's on hunger strike or not. Tell pherm it's okay either way. Phe has to do what's right for pherm. Tell pherm I won't judge pherm."

Jesse feels a stab of pain as though a sword has pierced through her heart. Phe isn't going to tell her phe loves her. The frizzy woman is walking towards them.

"Time's up."

"I love you," she shouts as Ork is taken away.

26

Jesse cries on Artemis's shoulder all the way home.

"I want to get off here," she says between sobs, rising from her seat.

"But we're nowhere near home yet," says Artemis, looking bewildered.

"I just want to see the place one last time."

The girls get off the bus and walk down the back streets until they reach the fire exit staircase. Jesse knows nobody will be there any more, the place would have been raided weeks ago, but she just wants to stand there on the staircase and breathe the air in the spot they stood in together. Her and Ork. As the building comes into view, Jesse's breath is taken away by the huge mural of Ork's face painted on the side of it. Artemis takes hold of her hand.

"It's beautiful," whispers Jesse.

Artemis nods. "Looks just like pherm."

"It's not a memorial, is it?" asks Jesse, eyes darting to Artemis and back to the wall. "Phe's not dead yet!"

"It's not a memorial," says Artemis, her voice solemn. "It's a celebration of phers life and work. It's to show support for all phe is doing."

Jesse squeezes Artemis's hand tighter and they stand in silence, just looking, lost in their own thoughts.

When she gets in, she slams the front door shut, anger boiling up inside her at the sight of Randy's face, peering out from the kitchen, a sandwich in one hand. They haven't spoken since the police came. She couldn't bear the confrontation, couldn't bear the thought that her own brother might have made that anonymous call but now…

"It was you, wasn't it! I know you made that call!" she screams, flying at him and striking out, with fists and nails.

The sandwich falls apart, bread dropping to the floor, mustard splattering Randy's arm, as he tries to hold onto her wrists. But rage has made Jesse strong. He is no match for her. Her nails latch onto his face, claw out chunks of skin.

"Just admit it!" she screams, a woman possessed, her eyes fixing on the bread knife on the chopping board for one moment.

"Okay, okay! It was me. Just stop!"

Jesse stops and breathes deeply, murderous thoughts dissipating. She squares up to her brother. Standing at the same height right there in the kitchen, they are nose to nose, eye to eye.

"How did you know about us? Why did you do it?" she asks with contempt.

"I saw you two together."

Jesse stares at him. She's never been out and about with Ork outside the We Are One meeting place and the old school hall.

"When?"

"I followed Artemis one night after she dumped me. I knew there was someone else and I wanted to see them. I followed her to this place. I watched her go up some steps. I didn't know what it was. I waited until she'd gone in and then I crept up the stairs. The door was open and I looked in. I saw you with all those freaks. I saw you sitting on a sofa flirting with that, that…"

"Don't say anything stupid, Randy. Are you forgetting that you were no different a few years ago. You weren't always the big, macho man, you know? Or have you conveniently forgotten that?"

"I was never like that," spits Randy. "I might have had two sets down there," he says pointing to his groin, "but I was never like that up here," pointing to his head. "It's messed up. It's like Mum says, kids have to find their way. I found my way long ago. I'm nothing like those freaks!"

"Is that what you're so scared of, huh?" she shouts, watching the blood trickle down his face. "Scared that you might not be so different, after all? Make you feel uncomfortable do they? The Third Gender?"

"There's no such thing! I saw you with Ork, and I saw Artemis chatting to that other one, the one that got five years for chaining itself to the railings. I came back another time and it was just you two. I saw you…"

"Shut up! You don't know what you saw. You didn't see him raping me, did you?"

"Him? Is that how you think of it?"

"No, I don't. I mean, pherm! It's your fault, you've got me so mad."

"Firm?"

"It doesn't matter. You didn't see Ork raping me, you know you didn't. I don't know how much you saw but you must have seen that I was on top of Ork. I was the one making all the moves. Watch for long, did you? Enjoy watching your sister…"

Randy rears back and slaps her hard across the cheek, the sound reverberating through the kitchen.

"You're sick," he spits. "It made me feel sick watching you. I couldn't bear seeing you like that. Seeing you compromise yourself. I had to stop you."

"But phe's in prison anyway! What was there to stop!"

"I was angry about Artemis dumping me. I thought she was seeing the other one. I thought you two were in on it together. You always seem so cosy together."

"Artemis wasn't interested in Max. She didn't cheat on you. And even if she did, it would hardly have been Ork's fault or mine, would it?"

Randy falls silent.

"Does Mum know any of this?" asks Jesse, her voice small and hoarse.

She cannot bear to think that her mother had any part in it.

"No."

"Thank God."

"But she hates them too."

And that, realises Jesse, is the truth. It doesn't matter that her mother has a kind soul, wanting to help others, that she devotes her life to the cause of Natural Souls. It doesn't matter that she loves Jesse with all her heart. It doesn't matter that Ork wants a fairer world, equality for all, is trying to help make things better for future generations. They will never see eye to eye. Ork and Ana are not on the same side and they never will be. Jesse knows that her mother will never approve of a relationship between Ork and her daughter, will never understand the politics of We Are One. Not in a million years and certainly not within a lifetime.

She looks around the kitchen of her family home, photos of her and Randy and Ana on the walls. A picture of her and Randy on the beach, his arm around her shoulders, pink, sunburned faces grinning at the camera, her clutching a red bucket of stones that they'd spent hours collecting together. A picture of her on her mother's knee, sitting in the forest at the commune, green all around them, Ana in rolled up jeans and a white smock, Jesse in khaki, holding a bunch of twigs. The three of them standing together, Ana in the middle, hugging her children tight, snapped by Maya just before they started school. All these memories mean nothing. Not now. Nothing can be right if she stays here. She pushes past Randy and runs to her room, grabbing her holdall, the one she took to the caravan with Maya, stuffing it full of clothes, toiletries, random things. She pulls open her drawers and makes sure she has all her papers just in case she needs them. She runs out of the house, rushing blindly down the street. But where? Where can she go?

She takes her phone out of her bag. If she keeps it on her, they'll be able to trace her, she's sure. She just needs to get away for a bit to work things out. Ork is right. She cannot help him and stay with her family. She needs to be on her own away from her family, to work out what to do next.

"Maya?" she says to the voice at the other end of the phone. "Do you remember when you said I could always come to you for help? I need you now. Can you help me?"

27

"What happened? Where is she?" shouts Ana.

Randy hangs his head.

Ana is fifteen, hanging out of her bedroom window, long, blonde hair billowing, as she looks down at the garden, set for her brother, George's eleventh birthday. It hasn't changed that much since he was born. There's a patio where the weeds used to be and the old slide and sand pit have long been taken down and given away but the apple tree still drops rotten fruit over the lawn every summer, sticking to the soles of Ana's sandals and attracting the wasps. They have put a big table under the shade of the tree and covered it with a checked red and white table cloth. It is packed with crisps and sandwiches with food wrap still on them to keep the flies away, George's favourite Swiss roll and jugs of fruit punch. The weather is not as fine as they had hoped, a little choppy for a party, the edges of the table cloth whipping up into the air. The breeze blows through her ears, the wind chimes rattle in the trees, making her think of the triangle and tambourine that George still loves to play.

She pulls her head back inside the room.

Her mother is screaming. A primal, animal howl, like the foxes that Ana hears in the garden late at night. Ana has never heard her mother scream before, never even seen her cry. She is always so composed, always knows what to do, how to make things right.

Fifteen-year-old Ana bolts out of her bedroom and onto the landing, where she sees her mother's shaking back, standing in the doorway to George's bedroom, his beloved tambourine on the floor.

"You mustn't go in there!" bellows her mother, closing

143

the door and backing away. "You mustn't go in there! Stay in your room."

Her mother's eyes are wild as she pushes Ana into her room and grips the banister calling for Ana's father.

"P-e-t-e-r!" Her voice is shrill as she collapses to the floor.

Ana does as she is told. She doesn't go in George's room. But it is too late. She has seen George hanging by his belt.

"What happened? Where is she?" shouts Ana. "Where is my daughter? Where is Jesse?"

28

The fizz of the sea rushes over Jesse's bare feet. This time, she can go all the way in, not stop at paddling. She wades out, wearing a purple swimming suit, looking like any other young holidaymaker enjoying a hot, balmy day on the beach. Couples stroll hand in hand along the shore, or sit at beachside bars, sipping cocktails. Families with children play in the sand, building castles with moats and flags. Jesse jumps at the sound of a shriek. A girl with dark, floppy hair splashes at the water's edge, calling out in a language that Jesse is only just beginning to understand. Jesse never thought it would be possible to come somewhere like this but sometimes the impossible becomes possible. Guilt momentarily washes over her. For leaving her mother and Artemis behind. For not visiting Max before she left the country. For Ork, especially for Ork. Then the salty water rushes over her face as she swims and she is cleansed of guilt once more.

Jesse has stopped seeing her other half. He has disappeared for now but maybe he'll be back. Instead, she has started dreaming about her father and thinking about what Ork said that time. *You could probably track him down if you wanted to.* She doesn't know if she ever will but she likes to think it is a possibility that one day she will know her father and find out why he left.

Back on the shore sits Maya, waving, before standing up and heading back to the caravan. A different caravan from the one she took Jesse to all those months before, but a safe place all the same. Somehow Maya managed to get a work permit for them both teaching English, passports with fake ID. Jesse has no idea how Maya manages to do the things she does but sometimes superpowers do exist. She was cautious at first, sure that Maya would try to persuade her to go back home and talk to Ana. But Jesse remembered Maya talking about falling out with her own mother, about things not always being black and white, about people being more important than causes. She had listened that night on the phone, really listened, as Jesse blurted it all out between the tears, how she felt for Ork, what Randy had done, how her mother would never understand, would only condemn. And Maya somehow seemed to understand. She had been planning to get away by herself anyway – Maya never stayed in one place for long – and had no problem with Jesse tagging along, as long as they sent Ana a message to tell her that Jesse was safe and well and that Maya would look after her.

As she swims back to shore, Jesse puts her hand on her belly, still not quite believing it is true. The doctors still don't fully understand the rapid developments of intersex, can never accurately predict the fertility of any intersex couple. Of course, she doesn't know yet if the baby is Ork's or Zeus's. The scientific data would point to Zeus. After all, he is one of the Nine Per Cent. But something deep inside points to Ork. Nobody knows. Not yet.

Other novels by *The Red Telephone*

Calling for Angels

by Alex Smith

Em tries to avoid the annoying clones – the girls in her year at Philiton Comprehensive who spend all their time thinking about clothes, make-up and boys. She worries about her aging grandparents and her older brother Ollie, who seems to be behaving in a distinctly odd way.

Then three new people come into her life: the mysterious woman who gives her a beautifully carved figurine, Kai whose own story has a touch of sadness, and Zak, the new guy who causes a stir amongst the girls.

And she discovers she needs to call for angels.

Alex Smith is 16 and lives in Hertfordshire, England. She started writing when she was just four and says, "to me, writing is like breathing." She finished her debut novel, Calling For Angels, at the age of 14, "as a way of relaxing".

Winner of *The Red Telephone's* 2009 novel competition.

Order from http://theredtelephone.co.uk
Paperback: ISBN 978-1-907335-09-9
eBook: ISBN 978-0-9568680-5-3

The Prophecy

by Gill James

Kaleem Malkendy is different – and, on Terrestra, different is no way to be.

Everything about Kaleem marks him out from the rest: the blond hair and dark skin, the humble cave where he lives and the fact that he doesn't know his father. He's used to unwelcome attention, but even so, he'd feel better if some strange old man didn't keep following him around.

Then the man introduces himself and begins to explain the Babel Prophecy – and everything in Kaleem's life changes forever.

"It's thought-provoking and it's unique. I enjoyed it whole-heartedly, and will be looking forward to visiting Gill James' vision of the future again in the second Peace Child novel. Those who enjoy stories set in the future should definitely consider giving this out-of-the-ordinary tale a look." *(Amazon)*

"I was pleased to find out that the book is the first in The Peace Child Triology and I'll definitely be reading the next one!" *(Amazon)*

Order from http://theredtelephone.co.uk
Paperback: ISBN 978-0-955791-08-6
eBook: ISBN 978-1-907335-12-9

Babel

by Gill James

Babel is the second part of the *Peace Child* trilogy.

Kaleem has found his father and soon finds the love of his life, Rozia Laurence, but he is still not comfortable with his role as Peace Child. He also has to face some of the less palatable truths about his home planet: it is blighted by the existence of the Z Zone, a place where poorer people live outside of society, and by switch-off, compulsory euthanasia for a healthy but aging population, including his mentor, Razjosh.

The Babel Tower still haunts him, but it begins to make sense as he uncovers more of the truth about his past and how it is connected with the problems in the Z Zone.

Kaleem knows he can and must make a difference, but at what personal cost?

Order from http://theredtelephone.co.uk
Paperback: ISBN 978-1-907335-10-5
eBook: ISBN 978-1-907335-13-6

The Tower

by Gill James

Babel is the third part of the *Peace Child* trilogy.

Kaleem has given up the love of his life in order to protect her. He now lives and works on Zandra.

A sudden landquake, not known on the planet for many years, destroys many of the forests his father has planted to bring life back to the planet. The new relationship Kaleem has helped to establish between the Terrestrans and the Zandrians is also under threat.

A third party gets involved and Kaleem has to use all of his diplomatic skills to keep everything on track. Mistakes cost him dearly and he looks set to lose Rozia for a second time.

The Babel Tower mystery, others mysteries and sadness plague him. Can he find a way through to fulfil his role as the Peace Child?

Order from http://theredtelephone.co.uk
Paperback: ISBN 978-1-907335-29-7
eBook: ISBN 978-1-907335-30-3

www.ingramcontent.com/pod-product-compliance
Lightning Source LLC
Chambersburg PA
CBHW060934050726
47592CB00003B/944